Confessions from a

WINDOW CLEANER

Fucked in the Rear

Lloyd Smith

DEDICATION

To my son.
Jason, I know you are a massive fan of horror. I hope you enjoy reading this fucked up book as much as I enjoyed writing it. I look forward to publishing many more stories.
Love you always, Dad.

Prologue

Author

Lloyd Smith

Cover

Lloyd Smith

Editor

Omar Hassan

Note from the Author

Please be aware this book contains extreme violence, sexual violence, and torture, and may be upsetting to some people.
The book is intended for a mature audience.

Prologue

Buckinghamshire, England 2001

Scarlet lay in her bed listening to music on her headphones, unaware a criminal gang has invaded her home. Suddenly, one of the intruders wearing a balaclava, burst through her door. She has no chance to react as he immediately punches her in the face and he tells her, "Make a fucking sound and I'll beat your face in."

Another one of the intruders wearing a white mask with a black hood pulled over his head enters behind him.

"Please don't hurt me," Scarlet pleads.

The man wearing the balaclava strikes her hard with the back of his hand and tells her once again with a fierce tone, "I said don't make a fucking sound." The intruder wraps duct tape around her head several times making sure to cover her mouth; he then binds her hands behind her back with cable ties. He pulls the cable ties so tight her blood circulation stops at her wrist. The other intruder rummages through her drawers emptying the contents onto the floor.

He picks up a pair of her lacy underwear and says to his acquaintance, "We are going to have a good time with this bitch."

"You're a sick cunt," the man wearing the balaclava replies."

"What about the tag?" the intruder wearing the white mask asks.

"Not now, it will alert the law, when you are on the move you ditch it." As Scarlet is led from her room, she sees her little sister has woken and is heading down the stairs and the people abducting her do not notice the little girl and continue down the stairs with Scarlet. As they escort Scarlet through the kitchen, she sees that there are two more men, and they are assaulting her Stepmother and her dad. Her parents look seriously hurt.

Scarlet is led outside through the back door, and she is put in the back of a van and one of the men gets in with her closing the doors behind him. "Let's go," the man calls to the driver. The vehicle's engine starts up and they immediately head off driving in a calm manner.

The intruder that stayed behind removes his balaclava and heads back into the house, as he is about to enter through the back door Scarlet's mother bumps into him. She is forced back inside, and as she moves backwards through the door, she feels a hard blow in her lower back, and she collapses. "What the fuck," the man that has removed his balaclava says, "I said fucking restrain them while we get the girl; it's a fucking blood bath in here."

"Lizard, it came on top mate, I had no choice."

"Seriously Witty, fucking her wasn't part of the plan. Where's Tony?" Lizard asks sounding frustrated. Whilst they are talking Scarlet's little sister climbs out of one of the kitchen units and runs upstairs to her bedroom and she tucks under her bed covers to hide. One of the intruders enter her bedroom behind her and he sees the little girl tucked under her covers; she peeks from under her duvet, and he looks at her making eye contact, he smiles at her and she retreats back under her duvet. He closes her door and then heads into Scarlet's bedroom. He sets a fire by dousing her bed with lighter fluid then he makes his way downstairs. "Tony, hurry the fuck up," Lizard demands as Tony appears in the hallway. Rosie lay under her bed covers traumatised; she is paralysed with fear as she thinks the bad men are still there.

Meanwhile in the back of the van, Scarlet's muffled voice pleads with her abductors; she cries and prays that her family are okay. For a moment she thinks about her little sister, who is only four years old. Scarlet feels so

"Middle of nowhere," the driver replies.

"Cool, time to dump this bitch; after all, the slag fucked the both of us."
The driver agrees and whilst the vehicle is moving, he opens the back
doors. The rear doors swing open allowing the snow flurry to blow in from
the darkness. The vehicle continuously bumps up and down as it speeds
around the dark bendy country lanes, manoeuvring up down left right every
other second. The man takes a hold of an arm and a leg, and he throws
Scarlet from the moving vehicle. As she is thrown from the vehicle,
discarded like garbage her naked body tumbles and bounces on the ground,
breaking several bones and tearing her flesh before ploughing into a tree.
Scarlet lay unconscious naked in the blistering cold as the vehicle disappears
into the distance.

1

The Good Life

Buckinghamshire, England, 2001

An arm reaches from under the duvet to the bedside chest of drawers rummaging for the alarm clock. The clock continues a high-pitched sound and getting louder by the second. "Sam." She gives him a nudge. "How many times are you going to hit snooze?"

"Sorry, Hun." He swings his legs out of the bed covers and stretches his arms pushing all his energy through his fingers. He looks at the clock, "Shit," he curses under his breath. His eyes adjusting to the light, the alarm clock sounds again. Sam is a window cleaner, and he has less than an hour before he must meet his young apprentice at the tube station. His wife grumbles from under her pillow. Rubbing his eyes, he looks over to the figure tucked up in the duvet, his beautiful wife and thinks how lucky he is; he kisses her on the cheek, "Sorry Sophie, I love you," he gently whispers. His clothes folded placed on the windowsill, he gathers them and heads for the shower. Enjoying the feeling of the hot water he loads soap into his hands, covering himself in the foaming substance he smears it over his face obstructing his vision. He catches a glimpse of the door being closed and he steps out of the shower wrapping a towel around his waist. He opens the bathroom door and peers into the hallway; no one is there so he closes the door and proceeds with his grooming. Sam loads shaving foam onto his face and stares into the steamed mirror as he strikes his face with his razor.

"Daddy," the squeaky voice calls from behind him; he is startled, and he nips his lip.

"Sweetheart, what are you doing up." It is his little princess; he picks her up hugging her in his arms. She pokes at the blood trickling through the foam.

"Daddy, you're bleeding."

He taps her gently on the nose. "It's only a scratch sweetie, let's get you tucked back into bed." She smears the foam all over his face and chuckles and his heart melts. Sam puts her down and ruffles her hair, "Go on buttercup, go and tuck up with mummy."

"Okay daddy," Rosie replies as she looks up to him with puppy eyes; she then leaves her daddy to tuck up in bed with her mummy and Sam continues with his grooming. Now dressed he is more or less ready for the day ahead; he creeps down the stairs trying his best not to make a sound. Sam would normally indulge himself with a cup of coffee before leaving, but this morning after waking Rosie he thinks he had better not.

Rosie had not settled, hearing the front door closing she decided to get out of bed and go to her bedroom to wave daddy goodbye. "Daddy, daddy." She waves and knocks on the window. Sam is scraping the ice from his wind screen and his van engine is also running so he cannot hear her knocking on the window. Sitting in his van he enjoys the warmth of the heaters blowing warm air in all directions. The condensation on the wind screen now completely cleared he looks up to the large bay window where Rosie's bedroom is located and thinks of his family tucked up in bed. Sam begins to manoeuvre out of the driveway; as he is doing so Rosie once again appears at the window, missing him by seconds.

"Rosie," a croaky voice calls from the hallway as she enters Rosie's bedroom.

Rosie pops out from behind her curtains with a big smile and says, "I'm waving to Daddy, mummy." Rosie once again ducks behind the curtain to wave her daddy goodbye. "Love you, daddy," she calls out as she blows him kisses.

Sam having parked his van a short distance from Uxbridge underground station he waits patiently for his apprentice. He sips on a coffee enjoying the warmth of the cup on his hands. In the distance he sees his apprentice hurrying towards him. "Sorry Sam, the buses are ropy I think because of the cold weather."

"Don't worry Charlie, I was running a little late myself, and I just heard them say there are minor delays on the Met," he says reassuring him that it is not a problem on this occasion.

"Probably means it will be a mission getting home, Sam."

"Yes, I think you're right on the money, especially if this snow picks up." After waiting for half an hour for their train Sam and Charlie finally are on their way to the city. "Charlie, are you looking forward to tomorrow?"

"Not really, I'm not a fan of Christmas."

"No, why not?"

"Well, if I'm honest, it's because I'm not very close with my family, I was close with my Nan, but she passed away last year."

"So, what do you do for Christmas dinner?"

"I don't know, I might be able to have dinner at my girlfriend's."

"If you get stuck you can always come to mine, there is more than enough for one more."

"Thank you, Sam, but I don't want to intrude. Like you said, Christmas is for family, and you should spend it with yours." Sam thinks if only his daughter Scarlet had met a nice young man like Charlie.

Later

Scarlet moans and groans as she stretches in her bed waking from a deep sleep; she can hear voices coming from downstairs. She cannot clearly hear who they are, or what they are saying as the music that is playing outweigh the voices. The melody playing is one of Sophie's favourites, "Build Me Up Butter Cup." Scarlet sits up in her bed and wonders what the time could be. Feeling tired she grunts and growls, and suddenly her bedroom door burst open. "Scarlet, Scarlet," full of excitement, without taking a single breath in between her words, "Mummy's making cakes and I'm helping, and auntie Shann and Uncle Liam are here." Scarlet snarls springing onto her feet she ignores her little sister, and she quickly heads for the bathroom slamming the door behind her and locking it. Rosie pulls on the handle and pleads with Scarlet to let her inside. After another minute she gives up pleading with Scarlet and heads back downstairs. Scarlet now enjoying a hot bath she plays her music with the volume at full capacity with a thumping bass backing the lyrics.

Meanwhile, downstairs in the kitchen much happier music played on the radio. Sophie's long shiny blonde curls falling around her shoulders, all the way to her lower back and wearing no makeup she is just simply beautiful. She is wearing a pair of tight blue jeans, a fluffy white jumper a pair of fluffy slippers, and a cooking apron with a calming picture of fruits and flowers. Her sister is sitting on a stool at the breakfast bar sipping on a hot brew. Sophie's sister always looks at her sister in awe of her beautiful hair and wishes her hair were like it, unlike her own hair for whatever reason always just seems to look greasy. Boom, boom, the bass kicks through the kitchen ceiling. "Smack that Bitch," the only words they can hear below. From the bottom of the stairs she shouts, "Scarlet, please, how many times turn that off its foul." Back in the kitchen Sophie shrugs her shoulders with an open palm gesture.

"How is she now?" Shann asks, looking sorry for her sister. She continues, "Is she still pining over that scumbag boyfriend of hers? Has he been back? Since you know?"

"No, we haven't seen him since he done a runner, as for Scarlet I don't know what her problem is." She takes a deep breath. "All I know is we were a happy family before Kyle had arrived; I know there were issues but now, I don't know."

"You will be okay, you are a good family, and Scarlet has the best mum and dad anyone could wish for."

"Well tell Scarlet that, ever since she met Kyle, she constantly reminds me I am not."

"Shann, mark my words, this shitty teenage stage will soon pass and with Kyle out of the picture she'll look back and see how great you are and that everything you've done has been for the best."

Shannon sees her sister's eyes are beginning to well up. "Come on now don't get upset, I'm sure everything will pan out for the best, you'll see."

Scarlet suddenly appears and rudely interrupts, "You talking bout me, seriously Shann, I wish you'd stop bitching bout me all the time."

"Please Scarlet it's Christmas," Sophie pleads.

"Granddad and Ma over tonight ain't they?"

"Yes, they are so can you please be decent."

"They ain't the problem," Scarlet snaps back with attitude. Scarlet slides her feet into a pair of sliders that are placed by the back door and steps outside into the freezing cold. Wrapped in a pink fluffy dressing gown with purple glittery writing on the back that reads queen she lights a cigarette. Sophie and Shannon see her smoking and that she is texting on her phone.

Liam enters the kitchen with Rosie gripping onto his leg and tugging at his clothes. "Bloody hell, is she okay or what?" Liam asks sounding shocked by how rude Scarlet was to her mother and his wife.

"Don't worry," Sophie replies gesturing him to take the oven tray of baked fairy cakes.

Liam picks up a nearby tea towel and he takes the tray from her. "Mmmmm, they smell delicious," Liam says with a smile. "Can I have one."

Scarlet re-enters the kitchen letting in the freezing air followed by the excess smoke from her cigarette. She ignores Liam and heads back upstairs; within seconds, BOOM BOOM, the bass once again vibrates through the ceiling.

Cowley, West London, Later

"That was brutal," Liam says shaking his head. "The way she is so disrespectful to Sophie like that."

"Kyle, that's what done this. Scarlet was lovely until she got mixed up with him and his shit bag mates."

"I know Shann, he's no good for anybody; the sooner he's locked up the better off Scarlet will be."

"She will be eighteen soon, if she doesn't get her act together, she is going to find herself in prison."

Liam nods his head in agreement. "Just going to swing in here quick, we need some juice." As they make the turn into the forecourt of the petrol station, they could see at least half a dozen youths causing mayhem at the entrance of the store. "Fucking hell, look at them," Liam says sounding concerned, knowing this potentially could be trouble. "Some of them are Kyle's mates, aren't they?"

Shann shrugs her shoulders. "I'm not sure." Liam proceeds and pulls up at the furthest available pump from their line of view. "Are you scared of them?"

"No Shann, just don't want any unnecessary trouble."

"Kyle is not around, you know that no one has seen him in months, it would be too risky for him to come around here. He would be arrested." The group make their way to the corner outside the store. Liam gets out of the car and looks towards the gang of youths for one final check, and he hopes they will not recognise him. Satisfied they are paying no attention; he lifts a fuel nozzle and begins filling. Once the digital display shows thirty pounds, he stops and heads into the store to pay, keeping his eyes fixed to the ground. Back safely in the car he rubs his hands together. "It's freezing out there." He starts the ignition, and the car heating blows warm air all around. As they are exiting the forecourt, they come to a stop while waiting for traffic to pass. Their car stops directly next to the group of youths. Liam tries not to make eye contact with any of them as they wait. Shann's window being slightly open she cannot help overhearing their foul mouths as they throw abuse at each other and the public too. They are clearly drunk, with some of them holding bottles or cans of alcohol, and she also notices one of the girls sniffing something off a key. There are two men that look much older, in their mid-twenties. One of the men she notices has a scar on his face. People passing by are clearly intimidated; no one passes directly through the group. Liam exits the petrol station forecourt on to the main road as somebody on a moped pulls alongside the group.

2

Two Rotten Apples

West Drayton, West London, 2000

Kyle and Scarlet sit together on a bench by the local shops. They have just left a friend of Kyle's. Kyle is wearing a black tracksuit, his jacket is unfastened, showing a white t-shirt, and proudly displaying a gold chain. Scarlet is dressed provocatively wearing a white pair of skinny jeans and a black, white, and pink letter tape criss cross sports bra exposing the division line of her breast. It is nine-thirty in the morning, and they have nowhere to go. They are coming down from the all-night Cocaine session they have been on. Scarlet looks around at the concrete blocks taking in the scenery. The first leaves of Spring are appearing on the few trees that are on the estate. She looks up at the sky and notices a plane jetting across high above the clouds leaving a trail of two perfect straight white lines that gradually disperse into puffy clouds and she gives Kyle a nudge with her elbow and says, "Do us a line will yah." Kyle is in-grossed in his phone, and he ignores her request assuming he even heard. Scarlet nudges him again.

"What," he snaps.

"I want a little pinch in it."

"Fuck off, in a minute, not a lot left," he says sounding agitated and he continues to tap away on his phone.

Scarlet then draws her own phone from her pocket and after approximately half a minute, which feels like a lifetime to her, someone answers. Scarlet rises to her feet, and she walks a short distance from the bench. "Got some packet," she asks the person on the other end of the line. "Fucking prick," she curses with frustration. "He hung up."

She has now got Kyle's attention. "Who the fuck was that?" Kyle asks her agitated.

"Lizard."

Kyle takes a deep breath and shakes his head gesturing no and says, "You know you can't call 'em like that."

"Shut up man, he's always about yer know," she replies with confidence. "Sort me out then."

"Fuck sake, not out here," Kyle says as he points to one of the blocks.

Kyle and Scarlet are now inside the block stairwell. Scarlet offers her right hand as a fist and Kyle tips a small amount of cocaine from a paper envelope on to her hand; she blocks one nostril with one finger, and she sniffs the substance up the other. "Ah yeah," she says after tipping her head back giving one final sniff making sure to clear her nose. "Good shit." Kyle tips the remainder of the powder on to his own fist and sniffs the cocaine using the same method as Scarlet. "Fuck me," he says with a smile, and he takes a deep breath and starts to pant.

Scarlet looks at Kyle and sees sweat soaking his tee-shirt, "You didn't just do all that did yah? Fuck, that was half a gram there, you greedy fucker."

"Fuck yeah," he says, as he flicks a pea sized paper ball directly at her face. "Come on let's gel."

Before Scarlet has a chance to respond he has left the block. Scarlet calls out after him, "Where we going?" She follows him trying her best to keep up with his fast pace.

Kyle and Scarlet make their way to the closest bus stop. In the distance there is a sound of a commercial mower cutting the grass, accompanied with the most radiant smell that freshly cut grass gives. There is little traffic on the road and very few people are in sight, ahead of them they can see three young boys fooling around at the bus stop. Two of them are no older than twelve and the other is about Kyle's age. "Let's jux these fuckers," Kyle says as he cups his fist.

"All right then," Scarlet agrees, "Be a laugh." Kyle approaches the oldest boy from behind and as quick as a flash his arm is firmly gripped around his neck and with the boy's throat encased in his inner arm, he squeezes pushing the laryngeal prominence known as the Adam's apple inwards causing him to gag. The boy struggles and tries to escape and he swings his arms hopelessly not once hitting the target and then Kyle punches the boy once in his face making his nose bleed and then releases him from his grip. The boy drops to his knees coughing and Kyle looks at Scarlet and smirks. The three boys are so terrified by the violence they have witnessed, they stand frozen. Suddenly one of them make a run for it, "Grab 'em Scar," Kyle shouts. Scarlet attempts to stop him and he outmanoeuvres her and escapes; she does not give chase. With two of their victims remaining captive, Scarlet turns her attention to the youngest boy, who looks at the floor; his knees are trembling knowing there is no chance of escape. Kyle takes a hold of the older boy's hair and pulls him to his feet and sits him down on the bus shelter seat and orders the younger boy to sit next to him. The two boys sit terrified wondering what is going to happen next. "What shit you got, don't fucking mess me about, you get it, I'll fuck you up," Kyle asks them as he pokes the older boy repeatedly in the face with one finger.

"We have our phones, bus fare, nothing else," the boy replies with a tremor in his voice. They hand over everything they have, and Kyle passes their phones to Scarlet.

"What else," Scarlet demands. "This one's a piece of shit." She drops the youngest boy's phone on the floor and stamps on it repeatedly until it is broken beyond repair and then the youngest boy begins to sob. "Shut up, pussy," Scarlet says, poking him in his face. "Is that it, you are a little pussy."

The older boy interrupts, "Come on guys, we don't have anything else, let us go," he pleads. "We've done nothing to you."

Kyle chuckles. "Getting mouthy are yah."

"Why you picking on a little kid?" The boy bravely responds and pleads with them again to leave them alone.

"You wanna fight my woman do yah?" Kyle steps a little closer.

"Please, . . ."

Before the boy has a chance to finish his sentence, Kyle punches him on the jaw making a cracking sound as his fist connects, knocking him to the ground. Kyle looks directly at the young boy with a fierce expression and says, "Shut up, you whining little pussy."

The young boy's brother suddenly launches to his feet lashing out swinging his arms franticly trying his best to strike Kyle. "Run," he calls out desperately to his little brother. Kyle dodges his swinging arms as he ducks and dives like a boxer. Kyle responds with his own attack using a three-punch combination, a hook and jab followed by an upper cut; the boys head whips back hitting the bus shelter. He is punched with so much force his skull cracks the toughened glass, and he falls to the ground unconscious.

"Stop hurting him," the younger boy pleads.

In the distance Scarlet notices a bus fast approaching. "Gotta get out of here," she says to Kyle sounding anxious.

"Two secs, Scar." Kyle calmly begins to search Reece's pockets as he lay unconscious on the ground. He finds nothing and he removes the shoes from his feet ignoring his younger brothers pleads. He tosses the boy's shoes into the road for what purpose only he knows. Scarlet obstructing the young boy whilst Kyle searched his brother, stands aside. The young boy dashes to his brother's aid, cradling his brother's head he sobs. Kyle and Scarlet calmly walk away laughing and joking leaving their victims feeling humiliated. The bus arrives at the bus shelter and the rear doors open; only one of the passengers gets off the bus. "Oh my god," the concerned person says and hurries to their aid. The boy that lay on the ground unconscious opens his eyes, and he looks at his little brother and mumbles, "I'm sorry, Harry."

3

BLESSED

Badrick, AKA Lizard and his brother Joesph were born and raised in a rundown part of east London with a father that was an alcoholic, a prolific gambler and abusive to their mother.

Their mother again fell pregnant when Badrick was four years old, little did they know the baby was not their father's. Badrick felt helpless as he would listen to his mother pleading for mercy and he felt awful that he could do nothing to help her, and he would often lay underneath his bed covers and cry. Badrick was only four years old when he witnessed his pregnant mother being pushed down the stairs by his father; he watched helplessly as his mother lay at the bottom of the stairs unconscious. His father didn't even bother to call an ambulance. Badrick was found in the street crying by a neighbour and they called an ambulance, and she was taken to the hospital never to return home and what could only be described as a miracle her unborn baby was not harmed but unfortunately, she had a bleed on her brain and the doctors had no choice other than to give her an emergency caesarean. The baby was born premature and had to go in an incubator for a short time and their mother passed away from her injuries leaving her two-year-old and four-year-old sons without a mother; it was a tragedy. Badrick was heartbroken that he had lost his mother and he knew at that moment he hated his father and wished it was him instead of his mother that had to leave them. Badrick and Joe's baby brother was taken into child protection care where they would not get to see him until years later; with that said Badrick did get the honour of naming him. He named him Bennet, because the social worker that was involved at the time had helped choose a name and he told Badrick that the meaning of the name meant 'blessed.' He later became known as Ben. Badrick and Joesph also went into care spending their life in children's care homes and with foster parents. Badrick was a handful and found it very difficult to settle in any home. At school Joesph being a shy child and always nervous he was often picked on by his classmates; Badrick on the other hand was ruthless, he was the bully. Badrick would often skip school and he began shoplifting when he was ten years old. He soon moved things up a notch and burgled someone's home at the age of eleven. That was the first and last as he made little money for the risk and effort. Badrick soon began smoking cannabis before moving on to selling it.

Badrick was only thirteen years old, he was not too young to realise that there was potential in dealing cannabis to make money. He soon found himself in a young offender's prison at the age of fourteen for aggravated assault. He had gotten into a fight over a supermarket trolley with another child his age trying to claim one pound that had been left in it. It ended in tragedy as Badrick stabbed the boy in the face with a screwdriver blinding him in one eye. He was released eighteen months later at the age of sixteen and he became a runner for a local dealer running crack cocaine and heroin; from then on, he only dressed in the most fashionable clothes and would always have the most sought-after trainers, but this was not enough, he wanted more. So, at the age of eighteen years old he took over the dealer's round. To take it over he had to show him and other rivals he was not someone to be fucked with, so he beat him to a pulp and threatened to kill him if he ever tried to step on his toes. To prove how ruthless he was, he shot one of his runners in the face. He didn't kill him; he had the runner pinned on the floor with his pet bearded dragon stuffed into his mouth. With his foot on his head, he shot him through the cheek shattering his jaw and killing the lizard. From that moment Badrick became known as Lizard. He quickly grew a reputation as someone you do not fuck with. Lizard was feared in the local community and at this time he decided it was time his father paid for the death of his mother, and he abducted him and murdered him by tying his hands to his feet and his feet to a bag full of weights and he threw him from a bridge into the Thames whilst he was alive. Lizard never told his brother Joesph what he had done. His father just simply went on the missing persons list and has not been found to date. Joesph had managed to keep contact with Ben throughout his life, but Lizard's behaviour and reputation prevented him from being officially allowed to. Lizard would always buy him the best clothes and Joesph would pass them on to him. Ben had lived with two different foster families. He met his best friend, Charlie who lived with his second foster family before they passed away. They went to the same high school, and they were inseparable; Charlie was like a brother to him. A brother that was his own age and a brother he could talk to about anything, and he would listen and not judge him. Ben understood what it was like to lose your parents at such an early age. After the death of their foster parents Ben and Charlie were moved into the same children's care home as their social workers deemed it a good idea as they were so close, and Ben had been through so much.

Although Ben had grown up with two different foster families before moving into the children's home, he had lived a much better life than his older brothers; he wanted for nothing. His hair was always cut in the most stylish way, he was lucky enough to be able to dress in stylish clothing, he would always have a fresh pair of trainers every month and, most importantly, he had felt loved and had such a close friend whom he could count on. Ben was a popular kid at school and around his local area and people knew that he was related to Lizard so no one would dare mess with him. Ben did manage to keep himself out of trouble other than he once got a police caution for possession of cannabis after being caught smoking a joint.

Ben had just received his exam results and he had gotten good grades across every exam he had taken. His lowest grade was a C in humanities and his highest grade was an A star in Mathematics. He was on his way to having a successful life not involved in criminal activities. He had plans to stay on at school then go on to university if he was lucky enough to get a place. All he had to do was proceed with his schoolwork performing the same to get three Grade A results and he would have a chance. Ben had always dreamed of being involved in television; his biggest dream was to be a movie director. He excelled in a weekend drama school and was trying to get a place in full time but so far it hadn't happened for him. He was only sixteen years old, so he figured he had time, only his life was tragically cut short. His brother Joesph was overwhelmed with guilt for a long time afterwards as he had taken Ben and his friend Charlie to a squat rave and gave them ecstasy for their first time and after they left the rave, he thought it would be a good idea to take them to Lizard's to carry on the party. Little did he know he was leading his little brother to his death.

4

KILLING DAD

Hackney, East London 1999

Lizard's father sits slouching on a recliner chair watching a football game; he has a bottle of brandy perched between his legs and a can of high strength lager in one hand and a cigarette in the other. He hasn't a care in the world, or should we say he just doesn't care about anything in it. His wife is dead, and his children don't want to know him. He thinks about how his own life has been so tough and that if he was not treated so cruelly as a child, he wouldn't have such a short fuse and he would not have ended up an alcoholic. When he had his first son Badrick, he attempted to quit drinking for a short time until he got married; he was clean for six months and then he began drinking again even more so than he had done before. He also had a serious gambling habit and he found it very difficult to hold down a job because he would often show up smelling of alcohol and be regularly late. Within a few months of being married he started to control his wife's life. At first, she was not allowed to talk to another man without his say so and then he started to tell her who she can and can't be friends with. Eventually she was not allowed to leave the house without his permission, so it became impossible for her to go to work. Even before she fell pregnant with their second child she had had enough, but she was trapped, trapped in a relationship with a horrible man. The violence began with him pulling her by the hair and threatening to hit her and then he eventually beat her. The abuse just got worse with every day that went by. Two years into their marriage he raped her, and she fell pregnant with Joesph. After the birth of Joesph money was extremely tight so her husband allowed her to return to work on the condition she only travelled straight there and back and not to go or stop anywhere else for any reason without checking with him first and was to under no circumstances talk to another man. She was so unhappy in her marriage when a work colleague, another man began to show her attention, a kind man that often showed concern for her as he noticed she would sometimes be bruised. She eventually opened up to him and they became friends and they fell in love with each other and began an affair. She would ask her husband if she could work overtime as they needed the extra cash, she would convince him by saying if we are going to keep the heating on, eat and for you to have a flutter it needs to be done. Her lover gave her the overtime money and then they would spend the time together. For months it was going well and then she fell pregnant.

From the moment she knew she was pregnant she decided that is it, I am leaving him. With the support of her new man, she felt confident she could finally do it, but things didn't go as she had hoped. Her husband discovered she was pregnant, and she was no longer allowed to leave the house.

"How the fuck are you fucking pregnant, you slag," her husband screamed at her. "We don't even fuck."

"Please, I'm telling you it's yours. Look, you probably don't remember because you are always drunk," she replied with a trembling voice. Seven months into her pregnancy her husband found a cell phone that he never knew she had. The phone rang and he answered it but the person on the other end hung up. He then read her text messages, and there it was, confirmation, she and her lover had been texting each other and he read that she was planning to run away with him to have their baby. He was furious. "I'm gonna kill that slag and the rat inside of her." He confronted her with what he knew, and she begged him, "Please, I am so sorry, I promise the baby is yours." Her pleading and lying enraged him even more so he head butted her breaking her nose and punched her in the stomach and he dragged her up the stairs by her hair just so he could throw her down them.

Suddenly his doorbell rings and he snapped out of his thoughts. "Fuck off," he calls out and he turns the volume up on his television. He assumes whoever it is at the door is more than likely a neighbour complaining and has gone, then he hears a loud bang. As he goes to get up from his chair two masked men enter the living room. He looks at them, paralysed with fear and in shock. "What's this about?" he asks them nervously. They ignore him and one of the men leaps forward punching him in the face knocking him to the ground then the other man stamps on his groin and they both continue kicking him while he lay cowering on the ground. His hands are then bound, and a carrier bag is placed over his head, and he is led out of his home.

Southwark Bridge, London

"Please, I beg you, what's this about?" One of the men that have abducted him punches him hard several times in his face knocking out some of his teeth and causing his face to swell to the point he is unresponsive and unrecognisable. His feet are then bound together, and a bag filled with gym weights are tied to his ankles and both the men lift him from the car boot. One takes a hold of him by the ankles and the other grasps him under his arms and they both swing him until there is enough momentum to throw him over the side of the bridge. The two men hear a thud and the splash of the water as the man they have just thrown off the bridge hits its surface. "Lizard mate, I think your old man was still alive."

"I know Witty, it's only what the cunt deserves."

5

GONE SOUR

Hayes, West London, 2000

Kyle and Scarlet arrive at the home of the man known as Lizard, the roads are busy, the buildings are grey and drab. The area has consistent traffic clogging the streets and two high-rise buildings that look onto a busy road and a rundown housing estate with too little greenery to absorb the pollution. Lizards home is located on the sixth floor of one of the blocks.

Kyle and Scarlet enter the concrete tower covered with weathered blue cladding; they both notice what seems to be a homeless woman sitting against the wall by a door that leads to the stairwell. The woman is one of the many people that live on the housing estate with serious alcohol and drug issues. "Fuckin crack head," Kyle and Scarlet say simultaneously. They give no bother and make their way to the elevators. Kyle and Scarlet step out of the elevator and as they approach apartment six hundred and ten, they can hear a thumping bass echoing through the walkway. They continue ahead until they are both standing at the front door of Lizard's apartment; the door is slightly open. Kyle steps into the hallway entering Lizard's apartment, and he calls out, "Lizard, Lizard."

"Come in, fuck wits," a voice shouts from the living room. They both enter the apartment; the lighting is dim, red, and full of huge smoke plumes as if there were a fire. The smoke smells familiar to them, the air is filled with marijuana smoke, and as they approach the living room the scent grows stronger. The people inside are dancing or sitting huddled together and shouting over each other as their voices are drowned by the heavy bass. Lizard shows no regard for the other tenants that live in the tower block as the floor vibrates beneath their feet from the bass as the music plays at full capacity. They can barely see through the cannabis and cigarette smoke.

As they enter the room, everybody cheers. "Just in time," a man holding a bong in his hand says. "Want a puff on this," gesturing Kyle to take it as he repeatedly coughs.

"Fuck it, I'll have a go, mate," Kyle replies with a big smile.

"Sit here," Lizard gestures to Scarlet as he rises from his seat. Lizard gets up from his chair and sits on a bean bag with two girls that appear to be prostitutes. Scarlet scans the room to see if she recognizes any faces, and no one looks familiar to her except Lizard whom she has met on many occasions to buy cocaine. "Want a beer, Scar?" Lizard asks her as he picks one up from the coffee table for himself.

"Yeah, cheers, mate," she replies, and she helps herself to a can.

"I didn't mean to get rude with yah earlier, I was right in the middle of some ting," he says as he swigs from the can.

"No worries, not a problem," she says with a delightful smile.

"What you after anyway?" Lizard asks her before gulping down the can of lager he had just opened.

"Some packet, right on a come down," she replies, and takes a gulp from her beer.

Lizard shakes his Skunk joint to loosen its contents and he places it between his lips and lights it; he takes a lug drawing the smoke deep into his lungs and exhales a plume of smoke directly towards her. "I ain't got no packet, we've washed what's left, that's what's in dat bong," he tells her as he places his empty can back on the coffee table, and he then turns his attention to his brother Joe. Joe is wearing a Brixton fiddler black beanie hat with a red gold and green band wrapped around it, crowned on top of his dreadlocks. Sitting to the right of him is his little brother and his friend Charlie who sat in the middle. Kyle forces himself next to the young man making it a very tight squeeze. "After you on dat, brother," Lizard asks him before giving his attention back to Scarlet. "Want a puff on this."

"Yeah," she replies leaning forward to take it; Lizard takes one last lug and passes her the joint and his brother Joe offers Her the prepared bong. "Nah, I'm alright, mate," she says and shows him she has the joint.

"Dats ment to be coming my way broth," Lizard reminds his brother.

"Hold on, I ain't had a go, I was just gonna let the pretty lady go first," Joe says as he prepares to light it.

"She's with me, mate," Kyle interrupts reminding them that she is his girlfriend. Lizard's brother ignites the pipe ignoring Kyle's comment. "You never done coke like this, seriously it's no different than putting it up your hooter," Joe assures Scarlet.

"Rather not," Scarlet replies, and she turns to Lizard and asks him, "You got any ting else?"

"Got some pills, they're bangers, white speckle doves, ain't seen 'em in time."

"Is he on 'em?" Scarlet says referring to someone dancing on the balcony waving and shouting I love you to God knows who.

"Yeah Mon, I met him and this lot last night in Brixton, we all rolled back here for an after party; my brothers just got here, they been out in Shoreditch, in it." Lizard reaches into his pocket. "Just a couple left, you can have 'em on the house."

"Sweet, who is everyone anyway, he ain't gonna introduce me, is he." She is referring to Kyle who seems to have forgotten she is with him. He is totally wasted from the crack cocaine he has been smoking since they arrived, but before Lizard has a chance to respond a man bearing a big scar on his face offers his hand.

"I'm Steve, everyone calls me Pep." As they shake hands, unsure why, he instantly gives her the creeps. "This is my mate Billy," aiming his thumb over his shoulder to a man standing behind him; Billy leans over the sofa and offers his fist to greet her. "Out there, is Jason," pointing to the kid who is dancing on the balcony. "Jay, come in here, mate," Pep shouts over the voices and music. Jason comes to greet her; he is topless and sweating heavily, noticing Scarlet just like every other male in the room he is stunned by her beauty. Without hesitation he looks directly at her breast and says, "Your fit."

The comment is brought to his attention by Charlie. "What the fuck you say, mate?" Kyle asks him with a fierce tone, and without any warning he leaps up from the sofa punching Jason hard in the face knocking him to the ground and blood erupts from his nose.

"Boys, boys," Lizard calls out trying to calm the situation. Lizard and the two girls also vacate the room. The two girls that are Billy's and Pep's company head straight for the front door leaving it wide open. Jason manages to stand; under normal circumstances it may have been different, but being high on ecstasy gave him the strength he needed to escape the chaos. He leaves the apartment not far behind the girls. Scarlet leaps over the sofa ducking for cover as objects are carelessly tossed in the room. Tucked behind the three-seater sofa glass bottles torpedo overhead smashing on the walls behind her, it is chaos. The music suddenly stops as the speaker wires are disconnected from its device after being torn from its mount and thrown at Kyle. Holding a knife dripping with blood, Kyle side steps and the stereo goes crashing on to the Balcony. Scarlet tucked behind the sofa decides to make a dash for the Living room door. As Scarlet exits the door, she passes Lizard, and he is holding a baseball bat tightly clenched in his hands.

Lizard re-enters the room and sees that Billy has been knocked out and he lay sprawled across the coffee table. From across the room, "Help us, he's been stabbed," Joe calls out as he holds his t-shirt on his little brother's abdomen trying to slow the bleeding. He gazes into his baby brother's eyes and screams an agonizing wail as he cradles him in his arms. His little brother is gurgling blood. Joe looks around the room, "Call a fucking ambulance," he shouts. Lizard looks on at the carnage that has erupted in his home, unable to think what to do next. On his right there is a standoff between Pep and Kyle and to his left his youngest brother lay bleeding to death in his other brother's arms. He drops the baseball bat remembering his phone is in the kitchen. He dashes to retrieve it and dials nine, nine, nine. "Ambulance," he frantically keeps repeating. Lizard exits the kitchen with the phone to his ear, "My brother has been stabbed, he's only sixteen, please hurry, six hundred and ten Croxley." Before he can finish giving the details, Scarlet strikes him on the back of the head with the baseball bat that he had dropped. He stumbles and drops the phone falling to the ground face first. The operator remains on the line, "sir," "sir." Lizard props himself up, concussed and feeling confused and his vision blurred; he cannot focus where his phone is, although he can still hear the operator. Lizard looks around the room, with his vision blurred he finds it difficult to focus and he vomits on himself. Noticing Scarlet about to attack Pep, he wants to call out but just cannot find the strength. Pep is facing Kyle ready for his next move. Scarlet launches an attack from behind swinging the baseball bat, caught off guard Pep cannot react fast enough. The baseball bat strikes him hard in his face and blood squirts from his mouth and teeth dislodge from their sockets. Pep screams in agony.

Kyle bearing a knife he attacks Pep, and he automatically reaches out his hand for protection, and the knife penetrates through his hand. "Fuck," Pep screams. Kyle pulls the knife from his hand and Pep retreats sitting calmly looking at the gaping hole in his hand; he is in shock.

Kyle looks at Scarlet, they make eye contact and smile at each other. "Let's get the fuck out of here."

6

CALM BEFORE THE STORM

Cowley, West London, 2001

Sam and Charlie enter the petrol station forecourt missing Liam and Shannon by minutes. Sam notices a large group of youths hanging on the corner of the convenience store. "Are you sure you want to make this the end of the line, they look like trouble."

"I'll be fine, Sam; I need to get a few bits anyhow."

"Sam, if you're only getting fuel, I'll pay for you so you can get yourself home."

"Thanks Charlie, but I need to grab some bits myself."

"Okay, happy Christmas I hope you have a great day tomorrow." Charlie goes on and heads into the store. As Sam finishes filling his van, he sees Charlie leaving the store carrying a carrier bag. He decides to keep an eye on him for a moment to make sure he passes the group of yobs safely. Sam watches Charlie as he crosses the forecourt, satisfied he is safe he heads into the store and as he walks through the entrance, he brushes shoulders with a young man from the gang of youths.

"Pep," the young man calls with excitement, "Scarlet's old man just went in there."

"No way, how do you know it's her old man?"

"Don't matter mate, I just know it one hundred percent is, trust me."

Pep turns his attention to the boy on the moped. "Ross." The boy on the moped gives him his full attention. "Do us a favour mate, see that van," pointing towards Sam's van inconspicuously. "When he leaves, follow him, see where he goes, and if it looks like his gaff, you let me know."

"No worries, Pep," the boy replies giving him a thumbs up. He leaves the forecourt and parks around the corner and waits for the van that he has been instructed to follow. "Touch, we've been looking for that slut and cunt for time," Pep says with a wide grin. "Listen boys, look after your selves yeah, them beanies are bangers." He and Bill fist bump the group, and they part ways.

Ross sits waiting for the van to exit the forecourt. Darkness has fallen, the night sky is illuminated by the clouds threatening snow and icy winds blow through the open spaces. "Bout time." Ross spotting the van leaving the forecourt he follows keeping his distance. Sam unaware he is being followed heads home and his mind wanders as he thinks about his daughter Scarlet being arrested last year and how she had been bailed by the courts with conditions and ordered to wear a tracking device. He thinks about her court date for sentencing, being January next year, and can't help thinking at least she's avoiding being punished around the Christmas season.

Buckinghamshire, England, A Short Time Later

The dining table is decorated with a Poinsettia plant in the centre, its red and green leaves compliment the Christmas theme, surrounded with a large service plate with an already sliced beef wellington pie dish and various vegetables and plates of buttered pre-cut tiger loaf bread, two gravy boats, knives and forks wrapped in cream and white napkins, serving spoons placed next to a cream, gold, and white luxurious Christmas cracker. Sophie's finest crystal glasses are placed to the right, their bone-chinar plates which have the most beautiful, elegant design with hand painted enamel pictures from the Charles Dickins classic, A Christmas Carol.

Scarlet enters the room. "Come on Scarlet, we are waiting to eat, "her father says followed with a joke, "We all thought you had fallen down the toilet." Scarlet's Grandparent's chuckle.

"Excuse me mum," Scarlet asks Sophie. Scarlet calls Sophie mum for her father's benefit as he has asked her to do so; his mother and father are there as guests, a rare occasion.

"Okay everybody, help yourselves," Sophie gestures as she begins to serve Rosie's food for her. Everyone around the table begin to fill their plates.

Her grandfather asks her politely, "Scarlet, have you been behaving yourself."

"Of course, not a lot to do ere is there."

Her father interrupts. "Don't be rude, Scarlet."

"It's okay, son. I've got to say this food smells absolutely delicious, I can't wait to tuck in."

"I have to agree, this Beef Wellington looks splendid, one of my favourites."

"That's why we make it mum, especially for you." After finishing their meal, Sam and Sophie begin to clear the table and they wash the dishes together stacking what they can into the dishwasher. Sam's mother, father, and Rosie continue to the living room and Scarlet heads back to her bedroom. Scarlet lay down in her bed and puts her headphones on and she thinks about Kyle's text message earlier in the day and considers if she should tell her dad, but she thinks better not to.

Earlier.

Standing outside wearing her dressing gown and little else smoking a cigarette Scarlet feels the bitter cold and she thinks about Kyle. "Where are you." Kyle whom she has a court order not to have any contact with. She takes her phone from her dressing gown pocket, there is a text message from Kyle. "Shit, speak of the devil."

The text reads, "I'm sorry for all the bullshit I think about you all the time, I know you don't believe me, but it's true, I miss you loads, one and only."

"Bollocks," she replies to the text. "Fuck you if dats true you wouldn't have done a runner and left me to all the shit." The conversation continues, Kyle tries to convince her that he is genuinely sorry for what had happened and that he doesn't think he stabbed the boy that died and how he would love to come back to the area and prove his innocence, but the odds are stacked against him. She doesn't buy it and turns her phone off.

Hayes, Northwest London, Later

"What you want," a voice echoes from the intercom of Croxley house tower block. "It's Pep and Bill, we got some good news mate, can we come up." The buzzer sounds and they enter the tower. Five minutes later they are at his front door. "Smells good," Pep says with a cheeky grin, referring to the smell of Skunk cannabis. Unlike the last time they were at the property it is silent and has been redecorated. As they both enter the living room, they look around at the apartment's new luxury items, a fresh white leather sofa with crystal cut buttons imbedded in the fabric and freshly painted walls and hanging proudly as a centre piece there is a life size painting of the hip hop artist known as Biggi Smalls.

Lizard is sitting on a recliner chair with his feet up in front of a large television playing a video game with a cannabis cigarette wedged between his lips. "What you saying, boys," Lizard mumbles trying to hold on to the joint between his lips.

"We've found where that bitch cunt lives," Pep says sounding pleased with himself.

"No fuckin way." Sounding surprised Lizard pauses the game he is playing and gives them his full attention.

Buckinghamshire

Rosie having to say goodbye to her Grandparents is always the hardest part of them visiting as she only gets to see them twice a year. Sam's parents live in Cornwall and Sophie's family live in the Northwest London borough of Middlesex only twenty minutes away from where they live in Buckinghamshire. Rosie calls out with a great deal of sorrow, "Bye bye gran ma, bye bye pa." Rosie blows her grandparents kisses as they head off.

Richard and Valerie smile and wave and blow them kisses and they both call back simultaneously, "We love you too, sweetheart."

With Rosie perched on one arm Sam calls out goodbye again waving them off. "Bye, thanks for coming, see you soon." Sophie calls out as she too waves them off with one arm wrapped around her husband's waist. Scarlet remains upstairs listening to music through her headphones. Sam and his family continue to wave and blow kisses until his parents are out of sight before closing the door to escape the bitter cold.

7

THE LIZARD'S DEN

Hayes, Northwest London

Lizard stands before four men in his apartment; on arrival they are greeted
with a help yourself all you can sniff cocaine buffet, as he thought this
would be a good tactic to get them prepared for what he was going to ask
of them. Like many others on the estate and surrounding areas they are all
involved in serious criminal activity. They are well known for several serious
violent crimes. Their crimes have frequently appeared in many Local
newspapers, and two of them have featured on a television program called
crime watch; they are not well-respected gangsters, but they are known for
their brutality. From oldest to youngest, Tony known as pyro, he is twenty-
four years of age, he has a long list of criminal offences ranging from drug
possession, shop lifting, animal cruelty and arson, a crime he regularly
commits. He has never been caught, although he is currently under police
investigation for a terrorism incident. Tony once cost British rail hundreds
of thousands of pounds as the service was suspended for several hours due
to a fire he had caused. Tony had first made headlines for an arson attack
when he was only ten years old. To the left of him is Sonny, he is twenty-
two years old, is ruthless, and has only been released from prison a brief
time ago for sexual assault. Standing in the centre of them is Taylor, he is
eighteen years old, he never has a lot to say and often comes across as
awkward; he is truly a wicked person. He has a lengthy list of criminal

36

offences ranging from street robbery, possession of a firearm and aggravated burglary and rape. Standing next to Lizard is Mark, known as Witty, he is seventeen years of age, many people tend to like his bubbly personality when they first meet him until they get to know him better and learn of his dark side. Although he has never been charged with a crime, he has committed offences ranging from street robbery to beating people up for money and he helped Lizard murder his father and raped a fifteen-year-old girl after he had drugged her the year before that.

8

PYRO

Gerrard's Cross, July 2001

It is early evening, and the high street is busy, people are out enjoying the various restaurants and the local cinema pubs and bars. The locals have long anticipated the opening of this restaurant that is promising the very finest Indian cuisine. Inside the restaurant it is a calm atmosphere, there are couples out to dine, friend groups and families. The restaurant lighting has a blue tone and white interior painted walls with seating placed along two walls with table and chairs through the centre and the entrance faces on to the high street with large windows on one side.

"Good evening, madam," the man says as he greets his customers speaking with an Indian accent. "Can I take your name, please?"

"Smith, we have a table booked for four people."

"Yes Ma'am, this way." The waiter directs them to their table and sits them directly in front of one of the large windows. Once seated he hands all of them a menu. "Would you like some colouring in to do," he asks the two children; neither answer.

"No, thank you," their mother replies looking embarrassed.

"Do I look like I'm five or something," one of the children interrupts.

"Don't be rude, Clair," her mother snaps.

"Not to worry ma'am, I too have young children, I understand." The waiter looks through the window on to the busy street. He asks the family what they would like to drink. Whilst the children are making up their mind the waiter continues staring out of the window tapping a pen on his note pad. Suddenly, there is a blinding flash followed by the windows shattering and the waiter is blinded by shards of glass penetrating his eyeballs and he feels a tremendous weight smash into his chest, and he stumbles backward falling onto a table behind him. Panic spreads fast within the restaurant, some people head outside through the back and others scramble out on to the street. Most of the people remain in the restaurant either injured or in shock or too frightened to do anything; screams echo everywhere. The young teenage girl and her family sitting closest to the window have first degree burns as well as several shards of glass in their flesh.

A car parked outside the restaurant has exploded and many cars have collided, and a vehicle has mounted the pavement hitting a pedestrian. Some passers-by close to the explosion have been injured by fragments of glass and other debris; some members of the public stand in shock or stop to spectate the carnage that has unfolded before them while others rush to help injured people.

A brief time later the emergency service arrives, first the police followed by the fire brigade and then the ambulance crew. A large crowd has gathered to spectate. Within the crowd the persons responsible watch the mayhem they have caused. "Fucking Arab Cunts deserve it," Tony says to his accomplice with a cheeky smirk.

"Tony, think you might have gone too far this time," he says looking worried.

"Shut up dick head, don't get all wet behind the ears now, you wanted us to go bigger," Tony replies followed by a chuckle.

"We, that girl she ain't no Arab."

"Fuck 'em, they are in there eating their shit ain't they."

Within the hour the local press is on the scene and soon followed by the national media. "I'm out of here," his accomplice says sounding uncomfortable.

Tony stays to spectate loving the terror he has caused. He gave an interview to the press saying he was just walking by as the explosion happened. Within one month from the attack following a television appeal and investigation Tony was apprehended. Following his trial, he was convicted and sentenced under the Terrorism Act 2000, and he was served a minimum term of fifteen years in July 2002. He was released after serving eleven years in prison after the case was reviewed and he was deemed unfit to make rational decisions at the time of the crime due to his mental health. The parole board had now considered him harmless to the public after undergoing a series of psychiatric evaluations. By January 2013 he was a free man.

9

DISTURBED

As a young boy Taylor was sexually abused by one of his mother's many boyfriends. The abuse began when he was six years old. At first, he thought it was normal behaviour as his mother allowed it to happen.

He would never talk about it to anyone as he felt ashamed and embarrassed. He would often skip school and go to a local quarry where he would entertain himself by catching newts and frogs and he would then pull their legs off or cut other parts of their body to see how many cuts it would take until they died. One day when he was visiting the quarry, he stumbled across a little girl who was crying looking for her parents; she was only six and he was ten. He led her into some woodland, and he tortured her.

He was apprehended by the police who at the time said they had never come across a case that was so vicious and the perpetrator was so young. He went through the courts but as he was only ten years old, he avoided prison, but he was evaluated by a psychiatrist which led the authorities to finding out he was being abused.

He was taken into a children's care home and there he met Ben and Charlie. Ben never gave him the time of day as he thought he was a little strange but Charlie being such a nice person and always wanting to help people where he could he became the only friend that he had ever had. Taylor confided in Charlie about what he had done and to his surprise he remained friends with him.

Taylor then went on to sexually assault one of the girls that lived in the care home and as he had just turned eighteen the courts sentenced him to six months in prison with one year probation when he was released. In prison he was kept on a wing for sex offenders and there he met Sonny who was approaching the end of his sentence for rape of a girl at a music festival when he was eighteen himself.

10

PREDATOR

Isle of Wight, England 1996

The IOW Festival is world-famous and is a festival that draws tens of thousands of revellers every year. The weather is fine, and the skies are clear enough that if you were to look up you can see the stars. The party people are enjoying themselves to the maximum, and most of these revellers are either drunk or high on whatever substance they are taking. Most of the guys are topless and the girls in the crowds are wearing bear minimum clothing. Obviously, they are all here to have a good time and party.

For Louise this is her first festival. Adel is high on ecstasy and Louise has had one too many and is very drunk. Adel had bought the tickets for Louise's eighteenth birthday, mainly because she wanted to go herself; she thought it's about time her bestie had experienced something more than a house party. Adel being completely wasted from the drugs she has taken she has split from her friend and forgotten she's even there as she dances away to the music at the front of the main stage. Louise being very drunk she has wandered from the crowds to find a private spot to be sick. Louise is leaning on a tree in the shadows, she gags, coughs, and vomits where she stands. To her everything is moving in circles, she cannot focus, and she wonders where her friend might be.

"You ok there," a man asks her from out of nowhere, startling her. "Sorry, didn't mean to scare you, it's… I just heard you being sick, so I just wanted to make sure you are okay."

Louise leaning against the tree clutching her stomach she looks at the man with three faces and tries to focus and she says, "Thanks, I'm okay."

"Here, have a drink of water it will help you out a little, you are probably dehydrated."

She ignores her friend's advice not to accept a drink from strangers without seeing them buy it. "Thanks."

"No worries, where are your friends? Would you like me to call someone."

"My battery is dead."

"No worries, tell me a number and I'll call it for you." He dials a number and says, "Your mate said wait here, she'll be here in ten to fifteen minutes."

"Thank you," she replies, and she smiles with a sense of relief she is going to be reunited with her friend.

Meanwhile in the crowds Adel finally acknowledging she came with her friend she checks her phone for messages or missed calls. There are several messages from over two hours ago. The last one reads, battery is going to die soon, I'm sick. Adel immediately tries to call her; her phone goes straight into voicemail; she tries again and again. Adel's phone battery is also low on charge.

Louise is now barely conscious, and she has lost all awareness, she is in the middle of a field and lay victim to the stranger that came to her aid. Unaware and unable to move her limbs she was helpless as her clothes had been removed, she has been assaulted for the last hour, and the stranger proceeds to rape her.

Back at the festival Adel has been searching for her friend for at least an hour and is now beginning to panic. Her battery on her phone has run out so she decides to find a location where she can charge her phone and notify someone to help her find her friend.

Adel finally manages to find a place to charge her phone. She notifies security that she cannot find her friend and they tell her she is a big girl and that it is not their problem. She decides to head back to their tent, thinking Louise being drunk has more than likely headed back to sleep it off. When she arrives at their tent, she is surprised to find she is not there. Now Adel is really concerned for her best friend's safety. She decides to call the police and they tell her she is lost in the crowds somewhere and to call them back in the morning if she has not returned by then. Time passes by and later that night she receives a phone call from the police to tell her that her friend has been assaulted and that she is in the hospital, and she is asking for her.

Isle Of Wight NHS Trust, later

"I'm so sorry, I should have been there for you," Adel tells her best friend trying not to burst into tears.

"It's not your fault," Louise assures her. "Just don't say nothing to mum yet, please, I'll tell her if the police catch the bastard. Besides, I'm not sure I want this going to court, my name could end up all over the news. I've given a description the best I can, and police will get his DNA from the swab, they have also taken my clothes for evidence. I need you to bring me fresh clothes, and promise me you'll say nothing to no one, I beg you."

Within two weeks Sonny McKinley was arrested for rape as the police had already had his DNA taken from previous offences. Unfortunately, Louise being eighteen and in the eyes of the law an adult she was named in national newspapers along with her photo. She could not handle the shame and she later hung herself. Louise's body was found by her six-year-old sister and the story made headlines. Her family and friends were left feeling devastated.

Sonny went on trial which lasted nine months and he was convicted for sexual assault and sentenced to serve seven years in prison leaving Louise's family devastated once again and feeling cheated by the system as their daughter had lost her life. All because of that vile excuse for a human being.

Sonny was a free man after serving only four years in prison for his good behaviour. He was released on parole and put on the police sex offenders register and ordered to seek professional help for his sexual behaviour and within one month of being released Sonny sexually assaulted a fifteen-year-old girl and remained a free man.

11

Broken

Buckinghamshire, 2001

"It's freezing," Sophie says as she snuggles her body close to Sam's. His hands in his jacket pockets, the zip is unfastened, he wraps his arms tightly around her. Finally, alone in their rear garden, before them a small fire blazes brightly amid the snow flurry passing overhead. The fire lights up their faces and Sam and Sophie feel a sense of love and warmth between them, not due to the flames but for the love they feel for each other. Their little girl Rosie is tucked up tightly in her bed, after an exceptionally long day and late night. Scarlet has not been seen for several hours. Sophie gazes into Sam's eyes watching the flames reflect in his pupils and she says softly, "I love you," and she kisses him gently on the lips. "Rosie is out like a light; she was asleep before her head even touched the pillow," Sophie says still gazing into his eyes.

"I know Hun, she had a busy day," he replies as he rests his chin on her shoulder and presses his lips softly touching her ear and he whispers, "I love you more than this earth or anything on it." Wrapped within his jacket he hugs her tight making her feel warm and safe. Sophie gazes into her husband's eyes enclosed within his jacket and both their pupils dilate as a warm glow passes through their bodies and butterflies gather within their stomachs. She continues to kiss him softly on his lips. They kiss passionately; she cups his genitalia, moving her hand up and down until he has an erection. She unzips his trousers and slides her hand through the opening, she begins masturbating him. Unknowingly to Sam and Sophie two men have entered their home through the rear door.

Sophie leaps onto Sam wrapping her legs tightly around his waist. Holding her in his arms, her hands grasping his head they continue to passionately kiss. Sam carries her into the house, entering through the rear door he lays Sophie down on the dining table and removes his jacket followed by his other clothes that cover his torso. Sophie simultaneously removes all her upper clothing except her bra. Sophie unfastens his belt, and she passionately kisses him below the belt area and tugs at his underwear with her teeth.

Suddenly Sam feels the muscles on his back tighten, followed by spasms that course throughout his back and his chest tightens. A reflex response to the electric current that runs through his body, his heart races and he screams in agony.

Sophie sees standing behind her husband two men, one wearing a neck gaiter, sunglasses, and a black baseball cap, the other man is wearing a black balaclava. Sophie screams a deathly howl as her husband calls out in agony, two darts connected to a thin wire have struck his flesh, Sophie has no chance to process what is happening. Sam launches an attack swinging his fist wildly in all directions, he strikes the attacker wearing the balaclava. Sam suddenly feels his consciousness fade away as he is struck on the top of his head with a hard object by the intruder wearing the sunglasses and gaiter, blood squirts all directions and pours over his face. Sam drops onto his hands and knees and Sophie screams. She attempts to escape her attackers and scrambles from the tabletop. It is a pointless attempt. The man wearing the balaclava grips her by her hair and pulls her back forcing her onto the table. She kicks with both feet to keep the man away. The intruder manages to grip her by her ankles and she's pulled with extreme force from the table surface and her slender body crashes to the floor. As she attempts to rise to her feet she is punched and once again forced back onto the table. Sam positioned on his hands and knees, blood and sweat runs heavy like a flash flood over his face, he pants and gasps for air as the other intruder binds his hands before heading upstairs. Sophie lay semi-conscious on the dining table looking up at the intruder wearing the sunglasses. Sophie feeling the effects of concussion, she sees a third person wearing a white mask enter her home followed by another wearing a baseball cap, the visor covering his eyes. The four men look and appear to her like a bad nightmare, all she can think about is Rosie, and Scarlet.

Scarlet comfortably lay in her bed listening to music on her headphones, oblivious to the horror unfolding downstairs in her home; suddenly one of the intruders wearing a balaclava burst through her bedroom door. She has no chance to react as the man punches her in the face knocking her backward onto her bed. "Make a fuckin sound I'll beat your fuckin face in," the intruder commands with a fierce voice. She screams and he strikes her again across her face with the back of his hand. "I said, don't fucking make a sound."

Seconds later, another one of the intruders wearing a black tracksuit with a white mask enters behind him and begins to ransack the room emptying the contents of her drawers onto the floor. "Check the panties out," he says waving them in the air. "We are going to have a good time with this bitch."

"You sick cunt," the man wearing the balaclava replies as he wraps duct tape around Scarlet's head covering her mouth. He then binds her hands with cable ties and pulls her onto her feet. "Listen, when you're on the move you remove the tag and ditch it," he commands his accomplice. Unknown to them, Scarlet's little sister is standing in the hallway after being woken from the commotion, feeling frightened she runs as fast as she can down the stairs to find her mummy and daddy, missing the intruders abducting her sister by a split second. As Rosie enters the kitchen, she sees one of the intruders hurting her mummy. She hears the other intruders coming down the stairs with her sister, so she quickly hides in one of the kitchen units.

Two of the intruders suddenly appear with Scarlet holding her by her hair; Sophie can see she has been hurt and that her hands are tied. "Please, don't hurt her," she calls out desperately, and she is punched causing her to lose focus. Sam looks on in horror as his daughter Scarlet is escorted out through the back door, and he is powerless to protect her. His daughter has been taken and his beloved wife is being assaulted right before his eyes. He wants to do something, but there is nothing he can do, he is bound, outnumbered, and has a serious head injury.

Sophie lay on the dining table and her vision is blurred; her face is covered with blood, her vision begins to refocus, and she sees her own reflection in the lenses of her attacker's glasses. With one hand he holds her down gripping her by the throat and with the other hand he fondles her breast. "You play nice, or I will fuck you up you fucking bitch," he commands her. Sam looks at his wife helplessly as the masked intruder stands in front of his wife who lay on the table battered and bruised.

Sam sees her attacker pull her jeans down as she struggles to fight him off, and with a rush of adrenaline he manages to leap to his feet, with his hands bound behind his back, he lunges forward throwing himself on top of the foul human being attempting to rape his wife. Sophie lay beneath them both and the impact from the weight of the two men breaks one of her ribs; she screams an agonising wail and Sam and the intruder roll off her onto the floor. Sam being a well-built man he is more than capable and would fight to the death to protect his family but tonight, he doesn't have a prayer, his hands bound and having lost a lot of blood from his head wound the intruder quickly gets the upper hand.

The intruder stands over him and looks directly into his eyes then realises his glasses have fallen from his face, his gaiter too. No longer concealing his identity, his eyes widened with rage, he explodes into a frenzy and punches Sam repeatedly in the face and his blood sprays all directions splashing the walls. Sam passes out from the beating and the intruder looks around the kitchen and he spots a knife rack on one of the work tops; he chooses the largest knife and sits down on his chest. Holding the knife in one hand his palm on the blunt side, he pushes the blade as hard as he can on to his neck and with one big thrust, he slices his laryngeal prominence, the Adam's apple. Sophie screams with terror; with a sudden rush of adrenaline she overcomes her agonising pain and leaps from the table to make a run for the open door. As she exits into the garden, she is confronted by a man she has not yet seen; his face is exposed. Sophie is forced backward through the door into the house and feels a punch to her lower back. She stares into the eyes of the man standing in front of her and her tears flow as she drops to her knees and falls sideways.

Rosie manages to sneak out of the kitchen unit, and she runs back up the stairs and tucks herself tight under her duvet and sobs. She peeks from under her cover, and she sees one of the intruders, the man wearing the baseball cap and he looks directly at her and smiles. Rosie tucks herself back under her duvet trembling with fear. The intruder leaves her room closing the door behind him and he enters Scarlet's bedroom. He douses her bed with lighter fluid, and he then sets it ablaze.

Sophie lay sprawled across the floor; she has been stabbed, one of her kidneys have been punctured, blood gushes from her wound as she lay unconscious. "Fuck sake Witty, it's a fucking blood bath in here," Lizard says sounding furious. "Where the fuck is Tony?"

"Here," he calls from the hallway, and they all vanish leaving behind a family that will forever be broken.

A short time later

Cries for help come from an upstairs window from the burning house. "Oh my god, that's the little girl," one of the Neighbours calls out in concern pointing up towards the bathroom window. "Hold tight, help is coming," he calls out desperately trying to comfort her. "We have got to get in there" the man insists.

"We can't make it through the smoke, the fire brigade should be here any minute," another neighbour replies. At that moment, the police and fire brigade arrive.

12

Changed

West London, Spring 2021.

A colour palette of peach and green, this church wedding look has an edge with the bride's lime-green birdcage veil and the amazing floral designs. No expense spared Mark lifts his new wife's vale and kisses her on the lips. Clapping and cheers echo throughout the church.

Mark and Cindy had met five years ago at a mutual friend's birthday party. Cindy became pregnant within two months of meeting Mark. She had heard a lot of rumours that he was trouble, but he always seemed so kind and polite it was hard to believe. They fell head over heels in love with each other and after their first child was born, they decided to get married once they had raised the funds. Her father had not long passed away when she had met Mark and her mother was struggling to make ends meet so they could not rely on the traditional 'the bride's parents pay'. As for his parents he had never met them. Mark had spent his childhood in and out of children's care homes. He used to be a nasty piece of work; he was up to all sorts. These days he lives only for his family. He has not been involved in any criminal activities since he met Cindy. He was finally happy, and he felt that he was genuinely loved. Mark had been very fortunate to have never been charged let alone convicted for any of his crimes.

Four and a half years on from having their first child Cindy became pregnant once again, this time the pregnancy was planned. They both had a good job and now on their way to owning their family home. Mark was so happy with his new life; he was so grateful for it.

A few months after getting married Mark sits in his garden staring at his home, and he thinks back to his previous life of crime; he chuckles and thinks to himself how lucky he has been to always somehow escape the law. He begins to wonder if there is anything that could come along and change things, like a potential witness that may for some reason decide to come forward. He thinks back to the year 2001, how he had gotten away with murder, a murder that he now regrets. He remembers how he and others high on Cocaine had savagely invaded an innocent family's home and that two of the men that were with him that night had abducted an eighteen-year-old girl who was only meant to be used as bate to draw out Kyle, but they had their own plans and they raped her. He came close himself to raping her mother and murdered her father. He knows if his wife were to find out what he had done his new better life would most certainly be over. Now happy within his new life he vowed to himself he would never inflict such pain on anyone ever again. That was until his life was turned upside down after the obduction of his child.

13

Taken

Summer 2021

The Weymouth coastlines are filled with fun activities for families and plenty of family friendly bars and restaurants. The beaches are impeccable, and the waters within the bay are calm and shallow for a credible distance, it is an ideal destination for a fun-filled family day out. Just a few months after the ease of lockdown some businesses remain closed. The weather today could not have been better for Mark and his family as they arrive at the sea front. After a three-and-a-half-hour journey from their home, they struggle to find a place to park within a reasonable walking distance from the sea front. Approximately half an hour looking for a parking space his wife decides to have him drop them on the promenade and he alone continue to try and find a parking space. He pulls over on a double yellow line and helps his wife unload their bags and pushchair along with their children.

Half an hour later from dropping his family on the promenade Mark himself arrives at the beach front. He decides to stop in one of the bars along the sea front to buy himself a sneaky pint of lager before he heads over to the beach.

As soon as his feet sink into the sand, he takes off his shoes and looks for the snack hut they had arranged to pitch nearby. He spots the location, and he continues towards it looking to see if he can spot his family. He sees them in the distance close to the snack hut. His wife appears to be struggling with the wind shield. As he approaches, she calls for him to hurry along, "Mark, hurry up please, this thing is blowing all over the place and Tommy hasn't stopped crying."

"Sorry Babe, I'm parked like a mile away, I thought I was never going to find a space." The wind shield now set up his wife and son can settle. "Cindy while you're feeding Tommy, I am going to take Jamie to choose an inflatable." She looks at him in agreement and they head off.

Mark and Jamie walk along the promenade viewing the various stores. Mark spots a huge inflatable shark hanging amongst inflatable doughnut rings. "Look Jamie, that is a big shark." Mark holding Jamie's hand leads him to it. Jamie shows no interest and is persistent on his dad to buy an inflatable pink and white sea horse. "This is for girls Jamie, look at the shark, I think this will be the best."

"Excuse me," a beautiful woman in a bikini interrupts. "I disagree, I think your boy has made a good choice."

"Please Daddy," Jamie pleads looking up at his dad with puppy eyes.

"Okay, looks like I am snookered," Mark says as he stares at the lady trying his best to keep his eyes from rolling onto her breast.

"How old is he," the woman asks Mark as she places her hand on top of Tommy's head.

"He just turned four the other day," Mark replies.

"Well, he is lovely, you are a lucky man." She smiles and says, "Nice to meet you two." As she walks away Mark cannot help but look at her bum.

"Look mummy," Jamie says with excitement as he smiles with joy, he couldn't be happier with his inflatable seahorse.

"That's nice Jamie, but I don't think you needed a shark too, sweetheart."

"It's for me babe, but I'm sure Jamie will have fun with it too."

"Of course, Hun, just make sure you put plenty of sun cream on him before you go in the water and yourself too, especially after last time."

"Jamie is covered head to toe in lotion, we are going to head down to the water," Mark says to his wife who is tucked into their wind shield with their baby. "Okay Hun, keep a close eye on him, won't you."

"Of course," Mark replies to his wife as if to say don't be ridiculous. His baby brother Tommy is a new arrival, being only two months old; he stays tucked tight in his mother's arms as Mark heads off to play in the ocean with Jamie. As soon as they enter the water, Mark holding Jamie's hand, together they jump over the waves. This is the first time Jamie has seen the ocean let alone play in the waves, and he loves it. Mark sits Jamie on the inflatable shark and pulls him along. The float manoeuvres up and down and Jamie giggles with joy. After approximately half an hour of playing in the water, Mark decides he had better go check to make sure the rest of his family are okay.

"Let's go and build a sandcastle, Jamie," Mark says as he tugs on Jamie's hand. They head back on to the beach giggling with joyful smiles. Jamie chuckles as he rolls in the sand and Mark captures the memory and thinks, if only he had his phone so he could film this moment. From the corner of his eye Mark notices the attractive lady he had met earlier standing in the shallows watching them. Although Mark's wife is very attractive, he cannot help noticing her, she is very sexy. Her figure is one of the most beautiful he has ever seen and without meaning to he removes her bikini with his imagination. The lady approaches, keeping a short distance she smiles at Mark. "Can I help you," Mark asks her.

"I have your little boy's sea horse, I found it way out in the ocean," she replies with a soft friendly voice.

Mark responds with a cheerful smile. "I have my hands full, I'll come back for it, thanks." Mark turns his attention back to Jamie and picks him up. His son perched on one arm and the inflatable shark in his other hand he glances over his shoulder to take a second look at the sexy lady. He draws his eyes from her breast and makes eye contact with her. She smiles in return. He focuses ahead, working his way through the smooth warm sand, with every step taken he attempts to clear his eyes from the fine sand particles that are twisting and twirling so gracefully as performing a coordinated dance along the beach. Jamie tucks his face into his father's chest protecting himself from the sand blowing into his eyes.

 Finally, back with his wife he places Jamie down, he runs straight to his mummy. She is trying to feed their baby without being blasted by sand and at this moment could do without the attention of her little boy, so she gives him a castle bucket and spade and he leaves her alone and sits digging in the sand. "Mark, will you go and get us some drinks please, I'll have a tea," Cindy asks sounding agitated. "Take Jamie with you."

"No worries," he replies as he notices the beautiful woman again holding their inflatable sea horse, he is distracted by her amazing figure. The woman seems to be staring directly at him. He doesn't want to invite her over as he is unsure how Cindy will react to her beauty, and he does not want her to feel jealous he had spoken to her as it may cause an argument.

"Mark, did you hear me?"

"Yes, I heard you." Mark had not paid full attention to what his wife had said but he did not want to let on he was not listening. "Pass us my wallet please," Mark asks politely.

"It's in my bag, Mark."

"Don't forget my tea," she reminds him.

"Yeah, yeah, tea and ice cream," he replies still not paying attention. Cindy tucks herself as far back in to the wind shield as possible, as she attempts to feed her baby without being blasted by the sand. Mark heads off and Jamie stays behind engrossed building a sandcastle. Jamie suddenly notices the inflatable sea horse he had wanted that he did not get a chance to play with and goes to get it. Cindy unaware he was even left behind ten minutes later Mark arrives back with two teas and three ice pops.

Mark calls out to his wife gesturing for her to take her refreshments and he then realises Jamie is not under the wind shield. "Where's Jamie?" he asks her sounding concerned.

"You were meant to have taken him with you, Mark."

"Fuck," he curses as the colour drains from his face, and he quickly scans the area to see if he can see him nearby.

"Mark, please don't tell me you have lost our little boy," Cindy says with a serious look of concern.

"I'll find him, babe." Mark immediately runs off heading for the ocean. Trying his best not to lose his cool he calls out his son's name; he knows in a situation like this, fear and panic are their worst enemies. He heads off to find a person of authority, asking people along the way if they have seen a little boy giving his description. "He's only four years old, knee high, wearing a blue hat and a white T-Shirt." He frantically continues to search the beach carelessly kicking sand into the air as his feet wade through it. No one has noticed anything.

Jamie's mother cradles her baby in her arms as panic sets in, her fears overwhelm her, and she begins to cry as she imagines that Jamie may have drowned in the ocean. She thinks to herself, if something has happened to Jamie, I will never forgive Mark, how will I ever forgive myself, she wails hysterically. After half an hour of searching with a lifeguard on a beach buggy they call the police. The coastguard searches the beach coastline just in case he had wandered into the ocean. The police put all their resources available into the search to find him. Their efforts achieve nothing. Jamie has disappeared without a trace.

14

Two Hearts

East London, spring 2021

In the club good vibes flow, and it is not possible to see the dance floor; it is wall to wall with people dancing to the music. The music playing is Techhouse. Badrick works his way through the crowd, many people's hands are in the air waving them side to side and their bodies are moving like an uncoiled rope while other people are jumping up and down. Being six feet and two inches tall, his shoulder muscles are so large he looks as though he has no neck. Over the years he has gained a lot of muscle, most of it from the time he spent in and out of prison. He ploughs through the crowd with no trouble, people just clear the way, or they are simply brushed aside.

Badrick is not out for a good time, he is at work; he is a door supervisor. Once a big-time drug dealer he is now fast approaching the fifty mark and he tries to live life on the straight and narrow; his criminal activities are all in the past. Badrick is urgently trying to get to a fight that has broken out at the bar. He finally gets through the crowds; a colleague is already there, and he has his hands full and clearly needs some assistance. As Badrick approaches his colleague he is punched on the back of his head. Badrick intervenes striking the attacker on his neck. The man he struck stumbles and falls to his knees. Another man leaps towards him attempting to punch him; he blocks the punch with one arm and strikes him in his face with his elbow. The man drops to the floor as if his legs have vanished from beneath him. Badrick stands posed like a boxer waiting for the next attack, but no one is willing to step forward to take him on. The short stocky man with a stern tone says, "Fucking hell Lizard, I could have done that, I was trying to calm it without brutality."

"Yeah right," Badrick replies sarcastically.

"For Fuck's sake," the stocky man snaps sounding frustrated, "There's already way too many people in ere, now two customers knocked silly, what the fuck now when the pigs turn up."

"Come on Pete, what you expect me to do, he attacked you from behind."

"Fuck off Lizard, it was like a fly landing on my head look at them, they're just kids."

"Kids shouldn't be in ere, Pete."

Pete is not impressed by the comment. "You know what, why don't you do us all a favour and fuck off outa here," Pete says sounding angry.

"Come on Pete, I thought I was doing you a favour," Badrick replies keeping calm.

"Doing me a favour, trying shut me down more like, go on." Pete gestures towards the exit. "Fuck off."

"Come on Pete, don't be like that, what am I going to do for work, man."

"Fuck off," Pete snaps again before disappearing into the crowd. Lizard has no choice other than to leave so he figures that would be the best thing to do and that he would call him the next day when Pete has calmed down.

The streets are busy with people walking all directions most of them are drunk having finished drinking at the various pubs and bars they are looking for somewhere else to continue their night. Badrick makes his way through the busy streets thinking to himself how he could have handled the situation differently. His car a good ten-minute walk from his work place he decides to stop in one of the many bars on the street to get himself a stiff drink.

After drinking two brandy's Badrick heads for his car. His car is parked on a back street, so he decides to make a cannabis cigarette. He starts the engine and waits for his windscreen to clear. While he waits, he smokes his joint and he thinks to himself he probably shouldn't be driving as he has had two brandy's and has only been released from prison on license with conditions, not to mention the Cannabis cigarette he is smoking. He starts to head home and just hopes he will be lucky. He thinks he will just drive like a regular person, *I'm fine, two drinks are fuck all,* he thinks to himself. He makes a forty-minute journey in his car without any problems occurring. As he turns onto the estate in which he lives, he hears a thud on the side of his car. "Fuck," he curses, he looks in his rear-view mirror and sees he has knocked somebody off their bicycle. At first, he thinks he will just drive away, he cannot risk being caught drunk driving and high on cannabis. He sees the person hasn't got onto their feet and that they are looking his way. "Shit, they probably got my plate," so he decides to pull over. He unwinds the car windows to vent the car from the smell of the joint he had smoked and gets out of the vehicle. He approaches the person; he cannot help but notice it is the most beautiful woman he has ever seen. "Are you okay?" he asks the lady sounding a little nervous and hoping she doesn't notice he has been drinking plus a cannabis cigarette too. "I'm sorry, I didn't see you, you come out of nowhere."

"Not to worry," she assures him, she reaches out her hand gesturing him to help her to her feet.

"Honestly, I am so sorry. You know these days, don't want to . . ." he helps her to her feet. "You know I wouldn't want you to think I'm trying something dodgy." As he helps her up, he cannot help noticing how great she smells. "Hope you don't mind me saying, but you smell great."

She smiles. "Thank you." She looks him in the eye. "You smell interesting too."

"Yeah, ah." He looks and feels awkward, thinking she must be referring to the joint he has not long smoked. "OK, if you're good then, I'm outta here," and he dashes for his car.

She calls out after him, "Not so fast, I haven't thanked you yet."

He stops in his tracks and looks back at her. "Thank me," sounding surprised, "For what, I run you over."

She chuckles, "You didn't run me over, you knocked me off my bike, that's all."

He just stands frozen in shock, he thinks, *Why is she being so nice about this.* "Well, look if one should be saying sorry, it's me." He looks at her in ore as she walks closer to him. Seriously, I am so so sorry." As she walks closer, he cannot help but look at her breasts, he tries not to, but his eyes keep rolling back to them. "Look, I tell you what," he pauses and takes a deep breath, "I'll buy you a new bike, any bike you want."

Ignoring his offer she says, "You are the most handsome man I have ever seen." She reaches out and touches his face, she continues, "You have such a chiselled jaw and kind eyes."

Confused, he thinks to himself, *really?* And he says, "Funny, I was thinking the same about you."

She laughs. "You think I have a chiselled jaw."

"No, no, that you're the most beautiful woman I have ever seen."

"Thank you, that's very kind."

"Give it up, you must have men throwing themselves at you all the time."

"No, the only male that throws themselves at me is my cat."

Badrick chuckles. "Look, I don't wanna sound weird or anything, I know this is a strange moment." He pauses for a moment looking at the ground. "Is there any chance I could get your number. I mean, you know, get you a new bike, maybe take you out for dinner."

She smiles and answers, "Yes, why not, it's not every day I get run over and invited out on a date."

He returns the smile. "Take my number and miss call me." He tells her his number and she immediately dial it. "What is your name?"

"Grace, and yours?"

He does not think it is appropriate to use his street name, Lizard, so he offers his hand to introduce himself. "My name is Badrick."

She shakes his hand. "Nice to meet you Badrick, I look forward to hearing from you."

They part ways and he heads off thinking about the unrealistic moment that just happened. "Wow, unbelievable," he says to himself, "Can't believe that just happened." As soon as he gets home, he begins to search the internet to find her a new bike. He finds her one and immediately buys it, he then texts her telling her thank you for being so kind to him and a picture of the bike that he has bought her.

She responds saying, "I think it was fate, I can't wait to see you again, you are so handsome." He blushes and he cannot believe his luck.

Cambridge, two months later

Nestled on the banks of The River Cam, the Graduate Cambridge hotel is an idyllic retreat inspired by centuries of rich traditions, storied histories, and academic life. Unrivalled views, seasonal culinary experiences, and a cosy bar in the centre of the hotel are just a few of the things that make Graduate Cambridge unique. Lizard and Grace have had the most beautiful start to their romantic weekend away together. Last night when they arrived, they worked up a sweat making love for several hours. This morning they spent their time in the Leisure Suite, now after a romantic afternoon tea in the garden they head out to see the sights and maybe do a little shopping. Lizard and Grace exit the hotel lobby onto the street. "I'm just going to make a work call, Hun; I won't be a minute."

"Okay," He replies with a warm smile. Grace engrossed on her phone Badrick heads back into the hotel to get them another coffee. "How is it, are things okay."

She looks at him confused, "Uhm."

"Your work, my love."

"Yes, everything is great, they all wish us a wonderful time." They head off holding each other's hand, they look at each other in blissful happiness and both simultaneously say, "Where should we go first." They both giggle. "Wherever you would like, my princess."

"How about the Botanic Gardens, it looks lovely."

"Fine with me sweetheart, as long as you're by my side I'm happy." After a delightful day and evening out, they return to the hotel and enjoy another night of blissful love making. The following morning Badrick wakes up and the love of his life is not in bed next to him. He looks at the time. It is 9:50am, he thinks how odd as they had set an alarm for 7am this morning. They must be checked out by ten thirty. He wonders why Grace had not woken him. Just as he is about to phone her, he hears the door lock click and Grace enters sweating, puffing, and panting. "Sorry Hun, I just realised we have to checkout soon." He can see she has been out jogging. She looks as sexy as ever wearing tight leggings and a low-cut sports bra. "Why didn't you wake me babe."

"I didn't want to disturb you honey, and after all you are the one driving us home, and after last night I thought you probably could do with the sleep. I'm going to hop in the shower," she says to him seductively. "Would you like to join me."

"You don't have to ask me twice."

15

Trapped

Mark reads the latest text message from the person that has abducted his son. She is asking him to carry out a task beyond comprehension. She is demanding he kills an old acquaintance of his, also a man that has dangerous connections. The instructions read, "It must be at the location, if you do not comply, I will fucking skin your son alive."

Mark screams in frustration, "Fucking hell." At that moment he receives another message. It is a video showing his son sobbing, asking for mummy and daddy.

Another text immediately follows, "You do this, and I'll give you the location and you will be reunited with your son."

He immediately replies, "What guarantee do I have?"

She replies, "Play ball or I will skin him slowly, your call. Show me how much you love your son. Do as I ask, I will give you his location and it's over." He receives another message, a picture of their home, and a text message, "I will kill them too." Then another video. Mark watches in horror as he can see only the front gate of his garden and the cars parked outside his house. He can hear a voice talking to his wife, he hears his son Tommy crying in the background. Another woman is speaking to her. "Hi there, good morning my name is," and the video ends.

He once again screams in frustration," Fuck." he lashes out punching and kicking any object within his reach.

He then receives yet another message, "Play ball or you lose them all. The only guarantee you have is, you Fuck with me, I'll skin Jamie alive then cut off all his limbs, and burn his corpse and if I reach your family, I will chop Tommy into pieces and feed him to Cindy and leave her knowing you're a fucking rapist. Follow the instructions."

"Fuck, Fuck," Mark screams with frustration and anger. He has never felt so mush rage run through his veins in all his life. Mark begins to wonder if he can trust this sick bitch. He knows the answer is no. He considers contacting the police, but he knows if this person were to find out she is crazy enough to hurt Jamie. He knows he has no other option than to do as she asks.

A brief time later Mark contacts Joe, "Seriously Joe, no questions asked, please I beg you just come and see me, and I will explain everything. Please, I need your help."

"What's it about, Witty," he pauses. "You know I ain't getting involved in any dodgy shit."

"Nothing dodgy, I promise."

"It's about Jamie."

"What about Jamie, have you found out what has happened to him."

"No, please just meet me at the location and I'll fill you in," Mark pleads. "I won't ask nothing of you ever again. I am not like the old days, I have a family."

"If it's about Jamie, why don't you just call the police."

"I can't do that Joe, please, just meet me at the location and I'll explain, please, you know I love Jamie so much."

"Witty, I can't stress enough, I don't wanna be involved in any dodgy shit."

Mark begs, "Please, Joe."

Joe reluctantly answers, "If it is going to help you find Jamie, okay, I will be there."

Somewhere In England, 2021

"When can I see mummy," the little boy asks his new auntie as she taps away on her phone. "Soon little angel, soon as your daddy says it's safe to go home."

"I miss mummy, daddy too," the little boy begins to sob.

His new auntie, being the person that abducted him. She sits on a bean bag provided for the little boy cuddling his inflatable sea horse, his only comfort, and sits him on her lap and hugs him tightly. "Jamie, don't be sad," she tells him as she strokes the back of his neck and assures him, "You will be with them soon."

"I'm hungry," Jamie whimpers. Jamie is only eating one meal a day. Since Jamie has been in her company he has been locked in the same space, unable to leave. There are no windows. He has been kept captive on a canal barge for three months. The barge is always kept moored on the opposite side of the public foot path along a remote part of the canal in Buckinghamshire. The cabin he is being kept captive has had the windows boarded up. Jamie spends most of his time sleeping due to the sedative he is given to make him sleep. In the corner of the cabin there is a bucket for a toilet. He is left alone most of the time. She visits him at random times to give him a meal and supply him with drinking water that contains the sedative.

Cowley, West London

Joe arrives at the pub he was requested to meet Mark at. The pub once booming with business is now derelict. The ground floor windows are boarded up, the first-floor windows are mostly broken. Joe standing in front of the boarded entrance he decides to ring Mark. "Brov, what are you playing at, this don't look like a good place to meet." Looking confused he continues, "Is it a mistake." He listens to Mark's reply, "Around the back, are you sure mate." Joe steps back and takes a good look at the abandoned building, he thinks this doesn't feel right. "Okay Mark, I'm coming in." He makes his way to the back of the building to find the rear entrance. Joe enters the building and cannot help but smell the stench of urine. He scans the area around him looking for Mark. There is rubbish everywhere. He calls out, "Witty." The sound of glass crunches beneath his feet as he proceeds further into the building. "Witty," he calls out again. Joe looks to what used to be the bar that is now in ruins. Noticing a door near the bar he heads towards it. He thinks it looks like what was once the kitchen. He pushes the door open; he calls out again, louder this time, "Mark." Joe enters the room, and it is confirmed, it is what used to be the Kitchen. He notices another door and proceeds to it. "Witty," he calls even louder. Joe steps through the doorway. There is a staircase in front of him and the floorboards are missing. He calls out again focusing upstairs, this time as loud as he can, "Witty, what are you playing at mate." Losing his patience he calls out again, "Either come and talk to me or I'm out of here."

He gets no response; he decides he's going to leave and turns back on the staircase. As Joe passes the doorway into the Kitchen, he spots a reflection of somebody on the chrome panels in front of him. Before he has a chance to turn around, he feels a punch on his lower back. He stumbles forward slightly, and he turns around. "Witty, what the fuck," Joe feels the area where he felt the punch and he feels a knife is lodged in his back. He looks at his hand and sees blood. He knows that he has been seriously wounded from the amount of blood and pain. They gaze into each other's eyes. Joe is still standing firm posed like a boxer ready to take Mark on.

This is not What Mark was expecting. "Sorry, Joe," his voice tremors as he talks. "I, I, had no choice." Before he can finish his sentence Joe leaps at him with the fiercest look upon his face and he punches Mark hard in his face with his fist knocking him backwards. He stumbles and falls at the bottom of the stairs. Joe leaps into the air, his foot stomps hard on the floorboards where Mark's head was. Managing to roll out of the way Mark scrambles up the stairs. Joe having been stabbed in the back he leaves the knife in place as he knows if he removes it, he will bleed much more than he already is. Defiant and extremely angry he gives chase although he feels his strength being sucked out of him by the second. As Joe reaches the top of the stairs Mark appears out of nowhere, clutching a hammer he launches an attack from overhead. Joe manages to catch and grip the hand holding the hammer. They struggle at the top of the stairs; Joe continues to grip the hand with the hammer. They continue to struggle punching each other with the hand they have free. Normally Joe would easily overpower Mark but due to the blood he has lost and losing more by the second he is getting weaker. Joe misplaces a foot on the stairs, keeping a hold of Mark they both tumble to the bottom.

Joe lay on top of Mark, motionless, he mumbles, "Why."

With a tear in his eye, Mark tells him, "Sorry, mate." He begins to wiggle his way out from beneath Joe. Mark stands up looking down at Joe realising the knife has plunged deeper into his back. Mark stands looking at Joe as his pupils dilate and he watches as the life disappears from his eyes.

16

Love is all around us.

Badrick fell in love with her the first time he had laid eyes on her, he could not believe his luck; she was much younger than him, and he knew at that moment she was such a loving and caring human being and the most beautiful woman he had ever seen. She would always say the right things and she adored him. He had accidentally knocked her off her bicycle after driving home having drunk two brandy's and having smoked a cannabis cigarette. He couldn't have been sorrier and after her wonderful charm and forgiveness he asked her out to dinner, and she said yes. They began seeing each other regularly and he fell in love with her more and more as each day passed. She worked as a nurse and had a good family and she seemed to love him, and it felt genuine.

After just two days of being in a relationship together, they began to have the wildest sex. Badrick was head over heels in love with Grace, he had never in his life felt this way for another woman. "People have always wanted to talk," he says, "But they never seem to want to listen, but you listened." He kisses her gently on the mouth, "And I love you for it." She kisses him in return, a perfect kiss a soft lip lock kiss filled with love and passion. They gaze into each other's eyes, and he says, "I love you, Grace."

"I love you too," she looks away, looking down at the floor as though she has something to tell him but feels nervous to say it.

Badrick asks her, "What's up, what is bothering you?"

She gazes into his eyes then hugs him tightly and whisperers into is ear, "I'm pregnant."

Badrick smiles with delight and his eyes light up, "Seriously, you're having my baby," he replies with excitement.

"Yes, we are going to have a baby, be a family, just like you have always dreamed," she replies as she cups her belly.

Badrick leaps into the air with excitement. "Yes, I'm so happy, I'm going to be a dad." He immediately draws his phone from his pocket, "I've got to tell my Mum and Joe." He paces the room. "Joe will love this news."

"Not so fast, calm down Badrick." She hugs him and takes his phone. "Let's wait until after the first scan, make sure everything is good." "What do you mean, good?"

"You know, just be sure the baby is healthy, then we will arrange a family party and we tell them the good news together."

She looks into his eyes, and she cups his genitals, and she says to him in a seductive tone, "Come to bed." After what felt like hours of passionate love making, Badrick lay back in bed staring at his future wife to be and thinks back to how he had met her, he cannot help but chuckle to himself, all his dreams have come true. He cuddles up to Grace and there is a moment he wonders, *what have I done to deserve this.* It feels like a blessing from God.

17

Good to See You

Marleigh Apartments Cambridge

Situated just under three miles from the city centre and surrounded by green spaces is Kyle's home. Kyle sits slouching on a chair in front of a large television playing a video game. Kyle resides there as temporary housing paid for by the state. His thumbs manoeuvre at a tremendously fast pace around the hand controller as he smokes a cannabis skunk cigarette which is perched between his lips. His television's volume is turned up to full capacity. For his neighbour's either side and below him it must sound as if World War III is happening as machine guns fire and explosions shake the walls and the floor that is a ceiling to another tenant below his feet. It is early in the morning, and he has been up all night playing his computer games and sniffing Cocaine, so unfortunately for his neighbour's he has no interest in going to bed any time soon. He hears knocking on the door. "For fuck sake, fuck off," he calls out assuming it is one of the other tenants complaining again. They knock again and repeatedly ring the doorbell. He pauses his game and thinks he will have to tell them to do one to their face. Kyle looks through the spy hole on his door and he sees a beautiful woman wearing a uniform and holding a clipboard. The first thing he notices about her is her breast line; he thinks to himself, they are the best tits I have ever seen. She smiles knowing he is looking through the spy hole and he opens the door, and he smiles at the lady, and he says, "What can I do for you."

"Good morning, sorry to bother you," she says as she flutters her eye lids. "Are you happy with your current energy company?"

Instinct tells him he should tell her to fuck off, being attracted by her breasts and feeling horny he fantasises thinking of a scene he had seen in a pornography film. "Come in if you like." He gestures her to follow him into the living room. She accepts his invitation, and his imagination runs wild. She follows him in closing the door behind her and as soon as his front door closes, he feels something sharp hit the back of his neck. Unsure what has happened he swings around with his fist clenched ready to take on the woman. Taken by surprise he stands his ground and feels the back of his neck to check for a wound, but it does not feel serious and there is no blood. They both stand there just staring at each other waiting for who is going to make the next move. She has injected him with a sedative that usually takes effect within seconds but this time it seems to have no effect and she is caught off-guard as she attempts to take something out of her bag. He rushes toward her, and she quickly retreats backward; he manages to catch hold of her hair and he pulls her to the ground and kicks her hard on the head. He goes to kick her again and she stabs him in the foot with another needle, as he pulls his foot back, he attempts to punch her and she hits him with a hammer, smacking him in his face and blood sprays from his mouth as he stumbles backward. Knowing she has hold of a hammer and that she is prepared to use it he runs for the kitchen, and she follows. She manages to close him down and he swings at her with his fist, and she strikes his hand with the hammer as she manoeuvres out of the way and he then stumbles and falls to the floor. His vision begins to blur, and the room turns in circles. Positioned on his hands and knees, he reaches out to the lady with four heads, and she strikes his hand again with the hammer, this time the bones fractures. The sedative she injected him with is now starting to take effect and Kyle begins to lose consciousness and he lay face first sprawled on the hallway floor. She sits on her knees with his head positioned between her legs and she pulls his t-shirt over his shoulders. Kyle tries to fight off the sedative, but it is no use, even with all the cocaine he has taken the drugs she has given him are too strong for him to fight and she injects him again with more just to be sure. She then sits on his head looking at his bare back and she takes a chisel from her handbag and places the sharp end at the bottom of his spine, without any hesitation she strikes the chisel with the hammer and his unconscious body responds, jolting and spasming. She continuously pounds the chisel until she has severed his spine. His body spasms uncontrollably as he lay unconscious. She then positions herself sitting on his back and takes a hold of his hair with one hand and pulls his head back so that she can see his face. Now bearing a Stanley knife in the other hand she cuts, stabs, and slashes his eyeballs repeatedly until they are obliterated and his blood spews out from his eye sockets.

Suddenly the doorbell rings. "Hello, are you okay in there?" a voice calls from behind the door. She quickly stands with her back up against the wall on the door side and holds her breath trying not to make a single sound. The voice sounds like a concerned elderly neighbour; she must have heard the commotion. "I have called the police," she calls through the letter box. The concerned lady then peers through the letter box into the hallway and sees Kyle sprawled on the floor and blood everywhere. "Help," she calls out loudly.

"Fuck," the intruder whispers. She knows if she remains here much longer, she could either be caught by the police or potentially by a member of the public trying to play hero. She could possibly be kept captive in the flat until the police arrive. She makes her decision; she opens the door in a panic, and she injects the old lady with one of her sedatives penetrating her chest. She manages to catch the old lady in her arms before she falls to the ground, holding her in her arms she pulls her into the flat and lay her next to Kyle. She feels for a pulse on her neck, "Fuck, fuck, fuck no." The old lady is dead, this was not part of her plan, this lady is innocent. Forgetting she has Kyle's blood on her face she leaves her tools and calmly leaves the premises hoping not to draw any more attention. She makes her way down the stairwell and in doing so she passes some children playing and they stop and look at her like rabbits caught in the head lights. She then realises that she is covered in Kyle's blood, and she makes a run for it.

Later

The atmosphere of the murder scene is one of pure horror, detectives cannot believe what has taken place. The entire residence on the same floor that the murders took place are asked to leave their premises and the area is sealed off from the public, including entry to the stairwell for the crime scene investigators to preserve and collect any evidence. Police take statements from two potential witnesses that may have seen the killer leaving the crime scene. They gave an exceptionally good description. "I want as much CCTV checked in the area as possible," the police sergeant detective asks one of his colleagues. "See if you can spot somebody that matches the description we have."

"On it, we have already retrieved some footage from the entrance intercom."

"A female wearing a OVO energy uniform matches the description had entered the building at seven forty-five this morning."

"Good, call a news outlet and see if they can run the picture ASAP, I would still like any other CCTV footage so we can try and trace this person's movements before she arrived here." The detective holds an evidence bag containing syringes. "Get these checked out ASAP and tell the press the woman is important to our inquiries as a witness not a suspect."

"Okay Sir, I'll keep you posted."

18

Burned

West Drayton, West London, 2021

Black clouds hang over the Suburb threatening heavy rain, the local bars are closing and some of their customers are now out on the streets making fools of themselves. Tony looks out through the window onto the street and thinks about the gangs of youths that will be roaming outside. He gulps down the remainder of his pint of lager before heading outside. As he exits the George and Dragon, he lights a cigarette and looks up at the sky and he wonders if he will make it home before it starts raining. He scans the streets looking to see if he can spot any potential trouble; the area is notorious for prostitution and drug dealing so it attracts a lot of criminal activity. Across the street he notices a woman looking his way and she appears as though she is looking directly at him, he looks at the time on his phone and looks back to where the woman was standing, and she is gone. He thinks nothing of it and begins his walk home. Although he would love to jump in a taxi or catch a bus, he has exhausted all his funds drinking. He staggers his way through the high street being aware that he is vulnerable drunk and alone; he has nothing worth stealing but this does not stop him from being a target from some of the criminal youth gangs that could attack him just for their entertainment.

Tony just makes it back to the block of flats where he lives as it begins to rain. He enters the block and as the entrance door is closing someone else enters behind him and before he has a chance to turn around to see who it is he feels something sharp pierce the back of his neck. He swings around with his fist, ready to take on whatever awaits him. "Fuck, you bitch," he curses as he grasps the back of his neck dropping his guard. He stares at her intensely as he struggles to focus. It is the woman he had seen earlier standing across the street, suddenly he loses his balance, and he stumbles.

"Here, let me help you," the woman says calmly as she wraps both her arms around his waist to prevent him from falling.

Tony awakes and the last thing he can remember is that he was in the stairwell seconds away from home. He is suspended in the air held up by chains connected to large hooks that are penetrating through his hands and legs with smaller hooks piecing his nipples and around his waist. The pain is excruciating, he is naked and cold, and he has not a clue where he is. He attempts to look around but all he can see is the decaying ceiling above him and a large white box. He can feel he has something around his neck, and he calls out, "Someone help me." Then suddenly he is electrocuted from the device attached to his neck; as he moves his limbs, the pain in his hands, legs and nipples is intolerable.

He desperately pleads and the electric current in his skull intensifies before stopping. He then hears someone is nearby. "What is this?" Tony pleads, "This some sort of joke?" He feels a tingle down his spine as the figure comes into view. It is a naked woman; she has the most beautiful slender figure, and she is wearing a freaky mask. It looks like black leather, and she is wearing a pair of steam punk goggles that cover her eyes and the mouth has a zipper, the scalp has large needles poking from it and she is also wearing a dog collar with large metal spikes. "What do you want?" he pleads. She does not respond; she just stands motionless, and she looks up to the ceiling above him then back at him and back and forth again as if gesturing him to look up. Tony looks up realising she is gesturing him to look at the huge white block above him. He cannot work out what it is but what he does know, it is going to be bad. She walks away and he tries to follow turning his head as far as his neck will allow him. Leaning his head back he sees her walk over to a table in the distance. As she pushes the table, a work bench on wheels towards him he can see the various objects on it. There is a hatchet, a hammer, a wood saw, and bolt croppers.

"Please, I beg you, whatever it is, it's nothing to do with me," he says as he sobs being aware not to raise his voice as every time he does, she electrocutes him with the device around his neck. As he continues to plead, she puts on an apron. The apron is the kind of apron a grandmother would wear whilst cooking a meal, it is a lemon-yellow colour with a picture of fruits and flowers. She picks up the bolt cropper's ignoring his pleads and stands by his feet. Calmly she places the cutting part of the tool over the large tendon at the back of his ankle. The Achilles tendon, the largest tendon in your body. It stretches from the bones of your heel to your calf muscles. He feels the coldness of the steel on the back of his ankle, she grips the handles of the tool and holds the position, taunting him. His body begins to shake with fear. After a minute of listening to him beg she cuts the tendon, and he roars with agony. He once again feels the electric currents run through his veins. She places the bolt cropper's back on the work bench and picks up a large needle showing it to him. He cries and sobs, "Who are you?" She ignores him then thrust the needle into his neck injecting him with Amphetamine Speed. It is a powerful stimulant that keeps people alert. She looks up to the white box suspended above him. The white box is Polystyrene soaked in petrol. She picks up a large pole from the work bench, one end of it has a rag wrapped around it. She applies some lighter fluid to it and ignites the material. He sobs and pleads some more. She picks up a hammer from the table and strikes him hard in the face dislodging some of his teeth and then raises the flame to the polystyrene box and ignites it and it instantly burst into flames. As it burns the substance begins to melt and hot polystyrene rains down onto his naked body. Even after being struck with a hammer and some of his teeth being knocked out, he manages to scream out as the polystyrene melts parts of his flesh. She strikes him again with the hammer this time connecting on his chin and his jaw dislodges from its sockets and it becomes stuck to one side. The pain is so excruciating he tries to move away to stop his flesh burning. It is no use. Within a few minutes he begins to fade in and out of consciousness.

Tony reawakening, he feels wide awake and fully alert. The Amphetamine she has given him has taken affect. The pain he feels over his body is excruciating. He has never felt such pain. He had hoped it was just a nightmare. But unfortunately for him he is stuck in the same position. The woman has gone. He hopes and prays someone will come and find him. Hours pass by and she returns. This time she is fully clothed and appears like an average woman; she is wearing blue jeans, white trainers, a low-cut top, a leather jacket and a pair of sunglasses. She stands beside him holding a needle and she smiles injecting him once again with Amphetamine. "We don't want you nodding off now, do we babe," she says sarcastically. "Back soon," and she leaves again, leaving him in agony high on speed and unaware when she will return.

19

Butter Cup

West London, 2021

The day is bright and sunny after a sharp night frost, the cheerful glitter of the Autumn Day not keeping in line with the news. On the television mounted in the far corner of the pub, near the pool table a picture of the woman the police are looking for in relation to the murders of two people, one of them being a pensioner appears on the screen; no one on the premises are paying attention to the television. "I can't believe Witty's kid was taken, still haven't found him," Taylor tells the bartender.

"You want another, fellers," the bartender asks Taylor and his acquaintance politely.

"Yes please, Bob," Taylor replies. "Sonny, get 'em in, I'm going out for a snout."

Standing outside smoking a cigarette and feeling the freezing air he thinks back to the days that you could smoke inside. Every woman that walks by who he deems attractive he either whistles at or calls out an inappropriate comment. Suddenly to his surprise a woman that is much younger than himself or maybe a very well-kept middle-aged woman approaches him. She has the most beautiful eyes and figure to match.

"Hi, you got a light, please," the woman asks him as she places a cigarette between her lips.

Taylor smirks and lights the cigarette for her and says, "If you don't mind me saying, you have the most beautiful eyes I've ever seen."

"Not at all, thank you," she replies with a lush smile as she blows her cigarette smoke directly at him.

"What's your name?" he asks her with a wide smile. "My friends call me Buttercup."

Taylor smiles with delight. "I'm Taylor, my friends call me Tay." He offers his hand for a handshake and then he too blows cigarette smoke directly at her and he asks her," Can I get your number."

The beautiful lady looks at him and flutters her eyelids and replies, "Sure." Taylor smiles and creates a tsunami of wrinkles throughout his face. "Give me yours and I'll call you," she says as she twists her hair wrapping it around one of her fingers and without a thought Taylor tells her his number. Once she has taken his number she turns and walks away. "I'll be in touch, Taylor," she calls back to him.

"Look forward to it," he replies with excitement. Once again Taylor thinks to himself, *one way or another she's getting fucked.*

Windsor

Cindy's tears have not stopped since the abduction of her son. "I'll never get over this, Mark," she says as she tries to settle their crying baby. She takes a deep breath, and shouts at her husband, "I fucking hate you."

Mark pleads with her, "I'm so sorry, he's my son too don't forget, and it hurts."

"Fuck off," she screams back at him."

Mark tries to reassure her, "He will be found, I promise you."

Cindy snaps back "Fuck off, it's been three months."

"I know it has been far too long, but I'm telling you . . ."

he says as he grasps her by her shoulders and looks her directly in the eye, ". . . he will be returned to us safe and sound."

Cindy looks at him in despair and she lay Tommy down in his crib and picks up a cup from the nest table and launches it at him. He ducks and the cup breaks on the wall behind him. "How the fuck do you know that?" she screams. "Get out, you fucking bastard, I fucking hate you," and she begins to pick up any object manageable and throws them his direction. As the various objects are launched at him their four-month-old son cries louder by the second due to the commotion. Mark knowing there are no words or actions he can say or do to comfort her he leaves ducking and diving the objects.

Mark sits in his car alone thinking about the situation and he wonders if he should tell his wife he knows Jamie is alive. It would give her a sense of hope to know there is a chance of him coming home. Mark knows if he were to tell her or the police the person that took their son would find out, and they may never see him again as she has threatened to torture and kill their son if he were to do so. He punches his dashboard out of frustration and tears begin to flow; he imagines how he will kill the person that has taken his son.

20

Cool Guy

West London 2021

Billy, who is active doing his evening routine, selling and delivering cocaine, is heading for his local pub, where a customer is waiting for him. He feels pleased with himself that he has managed to sell a substantial amount and the night has not ended yet. He enters the pub car park in a Black Mazda MX-5, his music is playing so loud the bass vibrates his windows. He is wearing a pair of Aviator glasses and he thinks he is the coolest guy in town. As Billy enters the pub car park, he bibs his horn to get the girls' attention that are sitting in the pub garden, he continues past them and heads to the rear of the pub. Once parked he takes a small bag from his glove compartment and uses his car key to sniff some Cocaine and he then texts the person that is waiting for him to come outside; he waits a few minutes and then decides to go in.

He enters through the side entrance looking out to see if he can spot his customer. The atmosphere in the pub is vibrant and busy; he cannot see him, so he decides to get himself a drink. "Pint of Stella please, Babe," he says to the bartender serving him who looks young enough to be his daughter.

"That's four pounds sixty please," the young girl says sounding a little nervous. Billy pulls a roll of bank notes from his pocket, and he proudly displays to the young girl he has a lot of fifties, and he hands her one of them. "You new in here?" he asks her as he waits for his change.

She hands him his change, "About two weeks now," she replies. Billy then notices his customer trying to get his attention, a man is waving him over, gesturing him to come outside. Billy enters the beer garden at the front of the pub. The man is sitting at a table with four girls and another guy he has not met before. "Alright, Conner," Billy says raising his pint.

"Squeeze in, Bill," Conner says, and he introduces him to the girls he had just honked at a moment ago and the other man. "Here, go get them in will you," Conner askes one of the girls as he hands her a bundle of notes. "Get shots for everyone." Billy was planning a quick drop off but decides to stay put as this could be good business for him. A few hours later after several shots the group are all very drunk and eager for a party. "Who wants to go back to mine for a nose up," Conner suggests; they all agree except Billy. He has made Four hundred pounds whilst drinking with them and he doesn't want to lose his earnings partying with them. So, not caring for the fact he is well over the legal limit he parts with the group and heads for his car. Once in the car he sniffs another line of cocaine, and he starts the engine, and the bass music automatically plays and once again the bass vibrates the vehicle. As Billy exits the car park, he can see the group in the distance cheering and making a fool of themselves. He exits the car park the opposite direction and after driving for about a minute he must stop at a red traffic light; he looks in his rear-view mirror and he is startled. There is someone in the back of his car wearing a mask with a mouth that is a zipper and there are pins sticking out of the scalp. Before he has a chance to react the person sitting in the back stabs him in both sides of his neck with a needle. Billy begins to feel drowsy, but he doesn't pass out, probably because of the cocaine in his system. The attacker takes no chances after the last time and stabs him again with another needle and within seconds he slumps on to the steering wheel.

Billy wakes up and finds himself restrained to the back of his car. "What the fuck," he curses unsure how he got in this situation. Billy has been stripped naked and his right arm is cable tied to his left leg and his right leg is tied to the rear of his car. "Who are you, what do you want?" Billy asks nervously as he realises, he is in the middle of nowhere. It is very dark and cold. "I can give you money," he calls out desperately. "In the glove box, take it." The car revs. "Please, what's this about," he pleads with desperation. He wails, "Help, please somebody." Billy's pleas are pointless as there are no other people for a credible distance. The engine from his car revs louder as the driver taunts him lifting her foot on and off the accelerator. "No, why," he begins to sob. Suddenly the car speeds off dragging his naked body along the gritty road and his body twists and turns bouncing up and down on the tarmac and the vehicle speeds around a tight bend and his body ploughs through a brambles bush cutting and slicing him all over his body. The car continues to drive carelessly, and his flesh is torn from his naked body as he is dragged along and one of his elbows dislodge from its socket and a leg snap in half. Suddenly the car breaks and his body ploughs into the back of the car with such force he shatters his entire rib cage resulting in one of his lungs being punctured. He sobs and begs for mercy; he is in agony, his flesh torn and cut, and bones are broken. "Please, help me, someone."

Billy's life flashes before his eyes and he thinks if he were to be freed, he would believe in God, he is praying for his mercy right now, he prays, *please help me, I will become a better man.* The car engine revs once again, and the person driving his car reverses the vehicle over him crushing his rib cage. Somehow despite all the trauma and being barely able to catch a breath he is still alive, he just wants it to end, he no longer cares if he lives or dies, all he can wish for now is for the pain to stop. Without any warning this time with full throttle the car once again races off. The car reaches thirty miles per hour within seconds and the hand brake is pulled and the vehicle spins a full three sixty and the breaks are applied; his body breaks free, and his hand and foot are torn off from his limbs, and he his flung into a field. Billy lay in the field unconscious, and the person stands over his broken body and stares at him with glee waiting to see a sign of life, and there it is. Billy mumbles, "Mum." The masked person cannot believe that he has endured so much. The killer had thought without any doubt he would be dead. Showing no mercy, the last person Billy will ever see places one foot on his neck and beats him on the head repeatedly with a hammer until his skull is obliterated, blood, brains, and skull fragment splatter all over the killer.

21

Lucky day

Bethnal Green, East London, 2021

Pep patiently waits in his car scanning the area for a prostitute he has arranged to meet. He can see out of his tinted windows, no one can see in. She is ten minutes late and he is starting to lose his patience. He dips a key into a small bag of Cocaine and sniffs it up one of his nostrils. He looks in his rear-view mirror and sees a sexy lady approaching. "Wow." He has never seen a sex worker as fit as this one. "Hope she's for me," he says as he clutches his penis, and before he knows it, she is sitting in the back of his car. Checking her out in his rear-view mirror he is practically dribbling. "Jump in the front," he asks her as he rubs his erection.

"No," she replies.

"You want me in the back?" he asks her as he unzips himself.

"No honey, drive to Orange tree hill," she tells him as she clutches his erect penis.

"Babe, this is as good a place as any," he tells her with excitement.

She replies, "No, honey. . ." talking seductively. "I'm going to suck your cock like no other." She tickles the back of his neck with her fingernails and the feeling gives him goosebumps. "I want you to fuck me hard all over this car in and on it, then I'll let your big hard cock deep in my neck and you can shoot your bolt all over my face," she says as she rubs his erection.

"This is one hundred percent my lucky day," he says with immense joy. He feels overwhelmed from the thought of the sex he is going to have tonight, and he does as she asks and drives off heading for the location. "Pull up here," she requests Pep. He is smiling as though he has won the lottery; he cannot believe how lucky he is tonight.

Suddenly he feels two sharp needles penetrate the back of his neck and within seconds he slumps on to the steering wheel. Pep wakes up from the injections and finds himself cable tied to the steering wheel. "What the fuck," he curses as he tries to break free not noticing the prostitute is still sitting behind him. She remains silent until he notices her. Her face is now covered with a freaky mask, "What the fuck do you want?" he asks with an angry tone, "You dumb bitch, you fuckin know who I am."

"Yes," she replies with a soft-spoken voice, and she stabs him again with another needle.

"You bitch," he snaps as he begins to feel drowsy and his vision blurs.

She binds his neck to the head rest of the seat making sure not to fasten it too tight to kill him and she calmly tells him, "If you struggle you will be strangled." She reaches into her handbag taking out a Stanley knife and then she grasps his face and digs the knife deep into his forehead and starts cutting around his hairline. From his forehead blood decorates the windows and pours over her hand. She continues to cut working around one side of his face following his hairline. He tries desperately to break free as he wails but it is no use as she tightens the cable tie around his throat. Blood spills like a fountain from his forehead and the side of his face as his hairline has been cut to the bone. She repeats the procedure on the other side of his face.

"Please," he begs and sobs. She sits back and takes a deep breath and says, "Sorry, I didn't think it would take so much effort." She chuckles then grips his bloody forehead and begins to cut again from ear to ear under his chin connecting all the wounds. He passes out and she sits back and waits. When he awakes, he can't believe it, his heart sinks to his stomach that she is still there. He becomes delirious and begins to say random words. "Blue skies," he sobs, he is no longer the hardcore gangster he thought he was that nobody messes with.

She chuckles. To him her laugh now sounds deeper as though it were a man, but he knows it is the prostitute he had picked up. She leans over the seat and digs her fingers under his flesh and from his neckline she pulls on his flesh from the bottom of his face tearing his skin and ripping it from the muscle tissue. She pulls and pulls, and he pleads, "Please, mercy," he calls out in agony. She ignores his plea, and with a large carving knife she pulls on his flesh exposing the muscle tissue within his face and she pushes the knife under his skin as if she was removing the skin from a chicken and starts slicing separating his skin from the muscle tissue. She repeats the procedure on both sides of his face. He calls out for mercy; his calls are ignored, and he once again passes out.

This time she does not wait for him to regain consciousness and tears the rest of his face off with her bare hands. Not able to hear him breathing and motionless she feels his neck for a pulse. To her amazement he is still alive, so she sits back and waits for him to regain consciousness; after half an hour he begins to mumble, she can't make out his words, she doesn't care. His head remaining slumped he has not yet fully regained consciousness, still alive she is bewildered he has made it this long. She thinks back to the last guy she slaughtered. "Must be the coke," she mumbles accepting he is not going to regain full consciousness and with one swift movement she slashes his throat cutting the Carotid artery. Blood once again sprays all directions decorating the inside of the car.

22

Rescue

Mark races in his car heading for the destination he has been told his son is being held captive. He thinks about the possibility of his son being returned home alive and the thought helps him overcome the guilt of what he has done. He continues to press ahead, deciding not to contact the police as he figures, if possible, he could catch this psycho bitch and serve some of his own justice, then call the law. He imagines his reunion with his son, how his face would light up with joy when he sees his daddy has come to rescue him. He thinks about the joy Cindy will feel with his safe return and all will be forgiven, and that they will be able to move on with their lives, as a happy family. As he approaches the part of the canal where the barge is kept, the fire brigade and police are already there. He exits his car and runs as fast as he possibly can towards the commotion. "Please, no, no, no," he puffs and pants as his anxiety levels go through the roof. Mark enters the canal foot path, on the opposite side. One of the barge boats is up in flames, he can only assume it was the boat he was told his son is being kept captive. Mark tries to read the name on the barge among the thick smoke plumes surrounding it, he finally manages to read the name and his worst fears are confirmed. He screams a mighty roar and turns and runs back to his car. He attempts to call the number that has been sending him messages, but it is no use; the phone is either switched off or disposed of. He sits in his car holding his head in his palms and cries his heart out. "Jamie," he calls in frustration lashing out striking his window breaking it with his elbow. "I should have told the police, fuck, fuck, fuck," he screams a deafening roar. "I'm gonna fucking kill you, you fucking hear me, you're fucking dead, dead, fucking dead."

Hillingdon Hospital, West London.

"How is he, Doctor?"

The doctor takes a deep breath. "He's a little malnourished and dehydrated, Officer." The doctor pauses for a moment to gather his thoughts and then continues to explain. "We took a urine sample and found Benzodiazepines, a sedative. We have informed his mother.

"This is truly evil," the police officer says looking distressed, "He has been through a real trauma."

"By the way Officer, we found this USB stick in his pocket, it might be worth a look."

23

No Satisfaction

An abandoned warehouse in London.

Originally a floral distribution centre, the derelict building and others that surround it reflects the urban decay of the area, the windows are broken, and graffiti decorates the walls. There is 20,000 square feet of floor space spread across the three floors of the warehouse and the abandoned building sits in between two other abandoned buildings, situated on a failing trading estate with very few businesses remaining. "Please, please, I have money, whatever you want," Taylor sobs positioned on his knees. His hands are secured to the concrete floor with heavy duty anchors and through his calves just below his knees. He pleads, "Please, please, no more."

"This is fucking sick, fucking sick, fuck," Sonny screams in frustration, with his arms wrapped around Taylor's chest, his hands are bound, and his legs are spread apart, and he also has heavy duty anchors penetrating through his feet into the ground. Taylor and Sonny have no idea how they have become this living nightmare, all they know for sure is, they are fucked. The last thing they remember they were all about to have sex together. They can see a few yards from them another man is suspended by chains about six feet from the ground, it is someone they know. It is a friend they have not seen in a long time, Tony. He looks as though he has been badly burned and savagely beaten. Taylor is defenceless, supporting the weight of his best friend Sonny, they are trapped, bound together. In the background they can hear music playing, the same song has been repeatedly playing over and over, Build Me Up Butter Cup.

The sexy lady they thought they were going to have the best time with, stands before them. She is holding a skewer in one hand; she takes a hold of his ear with the other and pulls his head tilting it sideways and pushes the skewer through Sonny's cheeks. The skewer penetrates one cheek and exits through the other and then she repeats the procedure on Taylor. They are both naked and they beg and plead with whatever sounds they can manage under the current circumstances. They can only look on in terror as the woman they thought they were going to have sex with stands before them. She is naked wearing only a cooking apron with a calming picture of fruits and flowers and a mask with needles poking through the scalp, the mouth of the mask has a zipper and over the mask she is wearing a pair of steampunk goggles. As the music plays the sexy figure dances in a seductive manner. She takes off her apron displaying the curves of her slender body, and she proudly displays her large breasts with her erect nipples, her legs appear slender and sexy. She dances around her victims in a seductive manner, wiggling her hips and stroking her breasts, and bending over in front of them showing all her glory from her behind. Tony watches the whole thing unfold, having been kept captive in agonising pain and unable to sleep for six days.

The sexy lady from hell then approaches them and she chuckles and says in a seductive manner, "You liked that." She looks at her accomplice and says, "I'll be okay from here." The man then walks away and disappears out of sight. She picks up a large knife from the floor and smiles and takes a hold of Sonny by the hair pulling his head back as far as possible and slices his throat from ear to ear. Blood pours uncontrollably over Taylor covering his face, his blood squirts all directions. Sonny slumps onto Taylor and he desperately tries to hold his weight. Taylor's elbows are already buckling, choking on his own tongue. She cuts the tendons just above the elbow joint on one of his arms. He can take no more. Taylor lay on the floor, the inside of his mouth and throat cut by several pieces of glass and his best friend lay dead on top of him. Taylor is struggling to breathe; he can feel himself losing consciousness as he watches the woman he thought he was going to have sex with walk over to Tony picking up a hatchet from the table along the way. She places the blade of the hatchet on one of his elbows taunting him. She raises the hatchet stretching her arm upward as far as possible and she chops through his arm just below the elbow joint, blood spills from his arm onto the ground. He screams a mighty roar, and he once again feels an electric shock from the collar around his neck. His forearm hangs by itself and his flesh tears ripping his nipples from his chest as his body tilts at an uneven angle. She then picks up a wood saw and places the blade teeth on his waistline; he sobs and pleads for mercy, his pleas are ignored, and she begins to saw, cutting into his flesh. He wails as she continues to cut through his lower torso. After sawing several inches into his body, blood pours and squirts all over her as she manoeuvres the saw back and forth.

She then turns her attention back to Taylor and he too tries to plead as he gags and tries to catch a breath. She squats in front of him and removes her mask; she looks into his eyes and smiles. "How does it feel being fucked in the face?" She then takes a hold of one of his ears pulling it outward and she cuts it off with the saw, he wails, and she repeats the procedure on the other ear. She draws her attention back to Tony and slowly walks over to him, she places the blade of the saw on his neck and cuts through his flesh and muscle until the blade touches his spine and then with one swoop, she cuts the remainder of his head off with the hatchet and blood sprays like a fountain from the opening where his head was. The crazed woman keeps on hitting his head with the hatchet spreading his brains and bone fragments across the floor and over herself. She slowly makes her way back to Taylor; her face and body are covered in blood. She stands in front of Taylor and bends over placing her perky bum directly in front of his face and she licks her fingers and says, "What goes around comes around, I hope it was worth it." These are the last words Taylor will ever hear, she then hits him repeatedly with the hatchet breaking his head in to several pieces.

Four days later.

Mark is unable to knock on his own door to see his family. Knowing Jamie is alive and well and inside the house he sits outside in his car hoping to catch a glimpse of them. The USB stick that was handed to the police by a doctor at the hospital was viewed by the police and a warrant was issued for Mark's arrest for murder. Mark knows he could explain what had happened, that a psychopath had blackmailed him. It would make no difference; he would be charged for manslaughter at the very least. He also knows his wife now hates him due to the fact he knew Jamie was alive all the time and hadn't at least told her. She was heartbroken. Mark lights a cigarette and thinks of how he should have done things differently. How maybe if he had just informed the police, they would all be a happy family together now. But what if she had done the things to Jamie she had threatened. No, it was the right thing to do he convinces himself as he struggles to hold back the tears. A vehicle suddenly pulls alongside his; he looks round thinking it could be the police. His eyes widen and all the colours drain from his face as he sees a shotgun pointing at him. The person pointing the gun at him opens fire and the window shatters and the bullet enters through Mark's face and the back of his skull explodes from the inside out and his brains, blood and skull fragments decorate the interior of the car.

24

Love Kills

Badrick had earlier received a video text from an unknown caller, and he decided not to entertain it and immediately deleted it. Badrick prepares the romantic scene for the love of his life; he is head over heels in love and he is looking forward to raising his new son with her. In the past he had always had a short fuse and had gotten himself into a lot of trouble, but since he had met Grace, something had changed inside him. His life is finally going in the right direction. He closes his eyes, and he thinks about how he has lost his baby brother, his tears flow for a moment, and he feels regret for his past and he acknowledges that his gangster life at least played a part in the death of his younger brother who was only sixteen at the time and that he took revenge on an innocent family. He thinks, *Should I tell Grace; no, how could I tell her I have been responsible for the murder of an innocent man and the destruction of his family.* He decides to pour himself a Brandy and make a cannabis cigarette. He heads out onto the balcony and considers jumping to his death. *No, what would that achieve,* he thinks. He lights the joint and with every puff he takes he feels a little more relaxed about the situation. Once he has smoked his joint, he sweeps his negative thoughts under the carpet. He is planning to properly propose tonight, with no expense spared; he has bought the love of his life an engagement ring and was going to prepare a romantic meal. He decides to complete the task, as he knows he cannot change what has happened and what good would it do to leave his child without a father; he wants to be the father his own never was.

An hour later the romantic ambiance of soft lighting and candles that Badrick has prepared is what any woman would love to come home to. He has a string quartet playing softly in the background from the television. A bottle of sparkling water and two glasses sit on the table he has prepared. He is unexpectedly a true romantic being head over heels in love with this woman; she is sexy, warm, a lovely person and she is carrying his baby. He cannot believe his luck; he wishes his mum and baby brother were alive so they could see how happy he now was. He once again thinks back to how he had met her, knocking her off her bicycle on his way home from work one night, he didn't think for a second it would lead to this. Grace arrives much later than expected. He had made such an effort to make it so cosy and romantic and the meal he had cooked for them had gone cold; nevertheless, he welcomes her home with a warm hug. As she enters through the front door, she looks surprised to see the romantic setting.

"Thank you, this looks amazing, I'm sorry I am late. . ." she says as she opens her arms to invite him for a hug, . . . "It's a lovely surprise."

"You're a little later than I was expecting," he replies trying not to show how upset he is.

"Sorry honey, I got held up with unforeseen events."

"Yeah, I had some unforeseen problems myself."

"Anything you want to talk about?"

"No Hun, its nothing important."

"The table looks amazing, thank you." Grace sits at the table he has prepared, and he heads into the kitchen to warm their meal. He presents her with a first course, Stilton soup with buttered tiger bread and they tuck in. "I heard on the radio someone has been murdered sitting in their car, right outside his home and on top of that whoever shot him went into his home and murdered his family, one of them was only a baby."

Badrick is surprised by her comment and does not know how to respond. Feeling anxious he replies, "Really. "

"Yes really, on Vine Lane."

"No way," Badrick replies trying not to show his emotion from the feelings he had felt from the thoughts of his mum and brother.

"Yes, apparently a witness got the number plate of a vehicle driving away from the scene."

"A witness," he says swallowing his words.

"This soup was delicious; I cannot wait for the main."

"Thanks." He takes their empty dishes and heads for the kitchen feeling anxious trying to decide if he should tell her about his brother. After finishing the three-course meal he had prepared for them he kneels in front of her taking her hand and he presents the ring. "Babe, I love you, you are the best thing that has ever happened to me in my life."

Before he has a chance to pop the question she answers, "Yes, yes, I love you so much."

"Why don't you go and wait in bed for me, I'll have a shower and then I promise I will relieve some of that tension you're feeling."

"Sounds great," he replies with a pleasant smile. He waits patiently in the bedroom feeling aroused and excited for Grace to join him. She enters the room, with two glasses of sparkling water. "You look beautiful and incredibly sexy," he says with a huge smile and his pupils dilate looking at her beauty. She didn't try to hide her sex appeal and she wore clothing that left little to the imagination. Badrick thought to himself it was going to be one of them moments when love making lasted gracefully for hours. She passes him one of the drinks; the glass is filled with ice cubes topped with a slice of strawberry and a mint leaf. He takes it and says, "This looks delicious, babe but not as delicious as you."

"Drink up," she insists. He drinks about half the drink and places it on the bedside cabinet. She mounts on top of him holding her drink and tips some of it onto his chest then begins to lick it off; she then removes her lacy bra and picks up his drink and pours it over her breasts. "Now your turn." He obliges and he licks the liquid from her breasts. She climbs into the bed sheets with him and begins to kiss him on his stomach slowly working her way down and his eyes widen with excitement as he feels intense pleasures. Beneath the sheets she grasps his erect penis and kisses it softly.

Badrick suddenly feels he has been stabbed and immediately kicks her out of the bed, the sheets instantly turn red. He springs out of the bed with a lightning reaction. "Fuck." He looks down at what she has done, blood is gushing from his groin. She has stabbed him; the knife remains lodged in his groin between his testes and his bottom. The knife has penetrated the Perineum. The perineum protects the pelvic floor muscles and the blood vessels that supply the genitals and urinary tract; it also protects the nerves used to urinate or have an erection. He cups the area with his hands and blood trickles through his fingers; he is confused. Furious, he launches towards her, she escapes from the bedroom, and he gives chase. "You fucking Bitch," he calls after her as blood gushes from between his legs. She heads for the kitchen, and as she's about to open one of the kitchen drawers he grabs her by the hair and pulls her away. Having hold of her hair he smashes her face into the wall and blood erupts from her nose. He stops the attack and thinks about their baby. "Grace, the baby," he says sounding very confused with the situation. "Why?"

She looks at him and says, "Baby, what baby?"

He looks at her confused. "What do you mean?"

"I was pregnant, but I've fucking terminated the fucking vermin," she says with a fierce tone.

"What," he replies looking concerned and even more confused.

"Remember my family," she replies sounding as if he should know what she is talking about.

"What! Who are you?" he asks sounding very confused and shocked. Suddenly she lunges at him holding a knife and he smacks it out of her hand kicking her in the stomach with a front kick sending her crashing to the ground. Unfazed she looks up at him and smiles. "You just terminated your own son, not to mention your friend Mark and his family; you killed an innocent family you know, you fucking murderer."

"What the fuck," he says not knowing what the hell she is talking about. "Why are you doing this?" She rises to her feet and smiles and stands with her feet spread apart ready to attack with a look on her face that resembles a crazed flesh eating zombie and she says, "Because you are a dirty fucking rapist, and you don't deserve a family, that's why your brother ended up dead, because he was the same as you," she says referring to his brother Joe. He does not know his brother has been killed and he assumes she is talking about Ben. Badrick punches her in the chest, and she hits the back of her head on the wall behind her and stumbles forward falling on to the table he had prepared for them to eat. She lay on the table barely conscious and Badrick mounts her, and he wraps his hands tightly around her neck and he squeezes. She tries desperately to grab various objects from the table to use as a weapon, she can feel herself beginning to fade. Suddenly Badrick's grip begins to loosen. The sedatives that Grace drugged him with are starting to take effect. She manages to pick up a fork and stabs him in the face, missing his eye by millimetres; he then releases his grip and climbs off her. Holding the side of his head blood trickles through his fingers and he stares at her laying on the table. She rolls off the table, rising to her feet; they are both naked covered with blood, and they look at each other in silence.

Badrick feels his knees wobble; he knows he is going to die from the amount of blood he has lost from the knife wound in his groin. He also knows he has been drugged and will not be able to put up a fight for much longer. He digs deep, and with all the energy he has left within him he charges at her. Tightly wrapping his arms around her he charges at the glass doors dividing the balcony with all his might keeping a hold of her tight within his arms he crashes through the glass doors, and they topple over the balcony railing. They plummet to the ground and are killed instantly.

25

Sorry

Shann and Liam are sitting together with their feet up with the company of their niece and close friend Charlie watching the television enjoying a cup of tea when the police arrive to give them the news. The police officers explain the horror that has unfolded and tell them that they should expect journalists at any time and that the story will most certainly make national news if not the whole globe. They are told that they will be expected to help them with their inquiries to tie up loose ends. Shann and Liam are left feeling devastated; they cannot believe somebody so close to them, someone they have raised and thought they knew had done all the terrible things the police had told them. They decide they have no choice other than to tell her sister as it will be unavoidable due to the circumstances. Without any doubt they think it would be better coming from them.

"Scarlet, honey," Shann kneels in front of her wheelchair and takes hold of both her hands gently stroking them with her thumbs. "Scarlet, I have some terrible news . . ." she says as she tries her best to hold back her tears. ". . . Honey, there has been a terrible accident, she pauses and looks up to Liam as he wipes away his tears. Shann looks into Scarlet's eyes, although she is paralysed and unable to speak, her mind is still functional. "Rosie has passed away."

26

The First Confession

"Before we get started, my name is John McDee, could you please state your name and why you are here," the interviewer asks the prisoner, surprised that the savage monster sitting opposite him looks like an average guy.

"My name is Charlie James Emerus, and I am here because I'm a serial killer."

"Well today's the day, how do you feel Mr. Emerus?"

"I feel great, pissed off that I'm in here, but overall, I feel great."

"Good, before we start, is there anything I can get for you, some cigarettes maybe."

"No, I'm fine, thank you."

"Okay Mr. Emerus, you are aware what you tell me today is going to be used to create a documentary, a documentary about you, and that it will air across the globe. How do you feel about that?"

"I love it."

"Great, Mr. Emerus."

"Please, call me Charlie."

"Thanks Charlie, now where would you like to begin?"

"Begin," Charlie replies unsure where to.

"Just talk about anything you like Charlie and we will just listen, this is your time," the interviewer tells him with a friendly smile.

Charlie slumps back into his chair and puts his feet on the table that divides them, his hands are cuffed, and two prison guards stand behind the television camera for the interviewer's safety. Charlie smiles at the camera, and he then starts talking.

"It was on Christmas Eve 2020 when I finally convinced Rosie to get the revenge that she deserved for the brutal murder of her mother and father and for the savage attack on her sister Scarlet that left her crippled. After her dad's murder, I became a self-employed window cleaner. I first took over her father's contracts and then over the years I have managed to build quite a lucrative business. Her father would often talk about his family when we travelled together for work."

"Her father was good to you; he gave you a job."

"I was only eighteen at the time and he would tell me how he had a daughter that was my age and how he thought she would be better off if she had met a young man more like myself. What he did not know is, I had met his daughter already the previous year. The day her and her boyfriend arrived at Lizard's I was there; little did anyone know I had a blade. I stabbed Lizard's brother just under his rib cage pushing the knife upward into his heart, knowing this would guarantee his death."

"Wow," the reporter stares at him intensely, "That is shocking."

"The best bit about it was, I was his best friend all the way through high school, so his family trusted me. My foster parents had taken him in, I had been living with them for about two years already when he arrived, he seemed to fit in really well and they adored him."

"And that made you feel jealous."

"I couldn't stand it, so I fucking killed them, when they went out one evening for dinner to celebrate their twenty-fifth anniversary of marriage, I followed them and then waited in a place on their route where there are no cameras and I caught them on their way home and I forced them into an alley way and then I fucked them up."

"I remember that case, it sent shockwaves through the community."

"I stabbed my foster dad in the stomach so he would be alive to watch me fuck his bitch wife up. I forced her to strip and made her suck my cock then I slit her throat. He cried his fucking eyes out the pussy, and then I slit his throat too."

John is amazed at the coldness as Charlie smiles and continues to explain.

"Their bodies were discovered that same night and we were notified by the police and for the life of me I was never a suspect, fuck knows how but hey, who gives a fuck I got away with it."

"The police had gotten DNA who they expected was the killers, and you managed to slip through the net."

Charlie nods his head in agreement as he chuckles, "We then later lived in the same children's home together because our social workers thought that would be a good idea, because he thought of me as his brother, I guess. His two older brothers Joesph and Badrick known as Joe and Lizard had always looked out for me. The whole room had already broken into chaos and Kyle had totally lost control like he had blacked out and gone into a fit of rage."

"So, what did you do?"

"I passed him the bloody knife and he continued on his rampage breaking things and lashing out on anyone that he felt were trying to hurt him; all he wanted to do was punch the boy that came onto his girlfriend to show the other guys he was not to be made a fool of. I knew these people were nasty pieces of work and it would not go down like that."

"And you calculated this on the moment?"

Charlie nods his head, yes, "Soon after he took the blade, I left Lizard's flat, no one had seen what I had done, all anyone saw was Kyle waving the blade covered in blood. When he used the blade on Pep, stabbing him through his hand it was perfect. Kyle being so wasted and having lost control even he believed that he had killed Ben. I loved it, this set all of what was to come into motion."

"The rape and murder of an innocent family."

Charlie smiles, "The other funny thing is I met this lad, Taylor, I became friends with him and as he had no others, so he one day told me he had tortured a girl when he was only ten; I thought fucking hell he is fucked up, I'll use him to my advantage later. So that is what I did, I figured when the moment arises, I'll take it."

"Yes, Talor was a troubled individual."

"He eventually abused a girl that lived in the same home as us and he ended up going to prison for it as he had just turned eighteen and had previous. I remained in contact with him to show him my support and build more trust. He only got a short sentence but, in that time, he met another sick cunt that was even sicker than him. Man, it was all so perfect."

"Perfect," John is now beginning to realise how cunning and evil this man is, "How is it perfect?"

"When Taylor was released, he introduced me to Sonny who had already been released and I got to play them both; a few times. I later introduced them to Mark who then introduced them to Lizard, and he got them in on the action. Lizard had no idea that they were convicted rapists. His friend Mark was a rapist too, he just hadn't been caught."

Johns jaw drops, "Lizard, is Badrick right?"

Charlie nods, yes, "The following year when Sam dropped me at the petrol station, I saw Pep on the corner with a group of lads and I knew he would go running to Lizard's. I could not approach them in front of Sam, so when I saw one of them in the store, I thought touch, and I tipped him off telling him who Sam was. The plastic gangster was only too happy to pass on the news."

"Sam trusted you."

Charlie chuckles, "I worked for Sam for a considerable amount of time, and he would often talk about me with his family."

"And this is how you learned about Scarlet?"

Charlie chuckles again, "He once introduced me to his sister-in-law and her husband, Shann and Liam. After the death of Sam and his wife I got talking to Liam one day about the tragedy that had took place, the tragedy that I helped happen."

"And how did that make you feel?"

"I loved it as he told me how his and his wife's heart was broken and that his niece had been savagely raped and left a fucking cripple and that they would be taking care of her so they could try and give her the best quality of life possible rather than her go into a care home. They also took full custody of Rosie."

"You loved it, being told his niece was paralysed?"

Charlie chuckles once again, "I told him that I thought Sam was a good man and that he had even invited me for Christmas dinner although he had only known me for six months. I told Liam if there is anything I can ever help you with please give me a call."

"I presume he did?"

Charlie licks his lips and for a moment holds a stern face, before chuckling again, "From that moment I became close with the family, and I watched Rosie grow. I would often volunteer to take her out for activities to help take some of the stress away from looking after her and her cripple sister."

"You became close with the family?"

Charlie smiles and looks him directly in the eyes and John looks away feeling uneased by his stare. "Later in her teen years Rosie began to show symptoms of being bipolar; this is because I sometimes spiked her with LSD, and other times I would confuse her by taking her things and putting them back weeks or months later. I would sometimes tell her a story then later deny I had told it to her the way she relayed it back to me."

"How on earth did no one notice she was being drugged?"

Charlie shrugs his shoulders and continues, "She found it difficult to make friends and to settle in school, but she knew she could always count on me, she looked up to me as if I were her big brother or even a father, I'm not sure. If she ever needed someone to talk to, I would always be there to listen; I understood her where no one else did, even Shann and Liam could not spare the time for her she needed as Scarlet required so much of their attention."

"They never felt any suspicion, they must have really trusted you?"

"Shann and Liam knew Rosie was troubled and would ask my opinion. I would tell them not to worry and I would be more than happy to seek professional advice and if they needed someone to accompany her to any appointments, I would be happy to be that person."

"And yet Rosie went on to become a nurse."

Charlie burst into laughter, "Rosie would often tell me how she'd like to be a nurse or a doctor when she grew up, so I used that as ammunition to encourage her to knuckle down at school; from her aunt and uncle's perspective, I was a blessing. Despite her mental health, which was created by me she progressed through school and went on to university."

"You wanted her to make it to university, but yet you drugged her with LSD to make her believe she was crazy, you could have jeopardised the whole thing."

Charlie shrugs his shoulders, "I loved her university days; I met a hard-line protest group called Black Lives Count, boy did I have fun with them, but that story I will tell you next time. Rosie eventually went on to training to be a nurse at St Thomas Hospital in London and after that she became a full-time nurse working at Hillingdon Hospital, it was perfect, access to drugs."

"So, Rosie becoming a nurse would later benefit you?"

Charlie nods with a smile and licks his lips, "Over the years I dripped the poison, implanting in her mind that the evil men that had raped, tortured, and murdered her parents should pay, that they should feel what they felt, an eye for an eye."

"Extraordinary."

"I would tell Rosie if you wanted the pain to stop you must serve your justice on the scum that had caused it."

"And she agreed?"

"Eventually she agreed, and my games advanced, I had hit the jackpot. I thought this is perfect, the wait was worth it, all of them years ago I not only managed to play the gang that had attacked her home and the two that had raped her cripple sister but now the ultimate. The only survivor: well, survivor that escaped in any kind of good condition that is. I made a bet with myself right then: I wonder, could I convince Rosie not only to kill the people that had committed these crimes against her and her family but kill them in ways that she could never imagine or think she was capable of; after all, if it wasn't for me her mother and father probably wouldn't have been killed nor her sister raped. Not to mention all the others I have played over the years."

"So, for you, the killing does not have to be by your hands, you get the pleasure from manipulating others?"

"But do not get me wrong I do like to get my hands dirty every now and again. I thought this would be a good challenge. She hates them enough to see them dead and she trusts me; yes, this is brilliant I thought, I am going to have fun."

"So, you had convinced Rosie, herself a victim to commit the most heinous crimes?"

"Along the way of her seeking her revenge I would encourage her that this is what needed to be done. I gave her advice on what she should do and made her feel we were a team, and a team we were. I let her conduct most of the work as that was important to me, but I helped with some of the matters."

"Can you tell me precisely?"

"I had taken Mark's son from the beach using the inflatable seahorse to bait him along with the help of Rosie's charm. It was funny really, when Rosie spoke to Mark and his son at the store where they purchased the inflatables, I was literally standing next to them listening to their conversation. The fact is Rosie was just there as a distraction and to ensure she would later take the full blame as she was the only stranger to have contact with them."

"So, you see all these people as pawns in your game?"

Charlie chuckles, "The barge where Jamie was kept captive on belonged to an old alcoholic man that people would avoid talking to as he was often rude and aggressive. I beat the fucking shit out of him with a hammer being sure not to strike a killer blow then strangled him to death on his boat and then I cut his body up into small pieces and I stored his body parts in vacuum sealed bags on the boat until I later set fire to it."

"So, what were your attentions for the boy?"

"My plan was to burn Mark's son alive along with the evidence; you know, any DNA I might have left behind when I killed the fucking whino, but hey, I suppose I can't have everything my way. Unfortunately, Rosie had a change of heart and had taken him to the hospital."

"Rosie had saved his life?"

"Although she had a change of heart with the brat, she still saw the rest of the plan through to the very end. Along our journey she sometimes struggled with some of the tasks so I would always be there to see them through; for example, I was the one that had abducted Billy and fucked him up. Don't get me wrong, she sedated him but then she had doubt."

"And what happened?"

"She called me and told me she was thinking of letting him go, so I had her meet me and I took over. I then drove him out to the countryside and man, did I fuck him up, it was awesome, he begged like a little bitch the cunt. On top of that when she met Pep, she went through with most of it but when I arrived to pick her up, she told me she couldn't go any further and that she thought he had suffered enough."

"What did you do?"

"I thought fuck that, so I went and sat in the back of the car until he regained consciousness, and I literally ripped his fucking face off with my bare hands and slit his throat. Man, it was fucking awesome."

John looks at the time and realises he only has a few minutes left for today's visit, "Tell me about the victims found in the warehouse in Hayes and how Mark came to murder Joe."

"I had set the cameras up to capture the footage of Mark killing Joe and posted a copy to the police, Mark's wife and Joe's brother Lizard."

"You played everyone against each other?"

Charlie chuckles, "I was also corresponding with Mark letting him believe that he was talking to Rosie. Not that he knew it was Rosie, but he did think it was a woman, the woman that abducted his son. I also helped Rosie get her victims into the warehouse and I secured them to the ground using heavy duty ground anchors that I smashed through their hands and legs."

John grits his teeth and Charlie smiles with delight.

"She couldn't go through with fucking them with the strap-on although she carried out the rest of it, so I took over for a moment and I fucked them with the strap-on. You should have seen the look on their faces when I appeared wearing it; they had known me for years."

John looks at the time again, although it is sickening what he is being told he can't help feeling fascinated by this twisted individual and is surprised how fast the time has passed.

"I had also set the polystyrene in place and soaked it with petrol. While she carried out the deeds in the warehouse, I stood back in the distance out of view and watched as I had a wank. I loved every minute of the show."

"You found it arousing?"

Charlie smiles and licks his lips, "When Lizard didn't react the way I'd hoped, I decided to take action myself and I shot Mark in the face outside his home blowing his brains out, then I thought fuck it, I'll do his family as well. It was all so perfect, and it only got better. His wife had opened her front door as I suppose she may have heard the shot; I was literally about to kick the door in."

"You had been so calculated over the years, what made you act spontaneous?"

Charlie smiles and bites his bottom lip, "She looked at me and could clearly see I wasn't there on friendly terms as I was pointing a shotgun at her, so as she ran back into her house, I shot her in the back. She was still alive, so I reloaded and picked the brat up by its leg and held it in front of the barrel of my gun and splattered it all over the fucking place."

John looks at the time again, with less than a minute to go, he doesn't want this interview to end right now even knowing he has access for another three visits.

"The bitch mother screamed like a scared little cunt then I walked into the living room and shot the other brat in the face blowing his head to pieces. Then as I left, I popped another one in her head. The best bit about that was, Rosie thought Lizard had done it."

John stares at him in disbelief, and Charlie feels a sense of gratitude.

"The fucked-up thing is she saw the plan through, and she had actually begun to develop feelings for him, and beggars believe she had fallen pregnant with his child, brilliant, two in one I thought. After seeing her pregnancy test and it was positive, I convinced her it was another illusion and when she had done a second one, I was prepared and swapped the positive one for a negative and I told her look again, see it's negative."

"You managed to convince her she was not pregnant, extraordinary."

"I think she knew deep down and the fact her period had stopped she was pregnant, but still, with the help of her imaginary bipolar I swayed her from the idea."

"So, not only did you convince her she wasn't pregnant, which resulted in the unborn baby's death, you killed a baby with a shotgun at close range?"

Charlie chuckles, "Rosie thought Lizard had killed a baby, so she was more than happy to kill him although she had feelings for him, and they ended up both falling to their deaths from his balcony."

"How did you find out?"

"When the police arrived to break the news to her uncle and auntie, I was with them. I got butterflies in my stomach; I loved it as I watched them break down. I mean after everything they had been through this was the icing on the cake. Shann and Liam having to tell their cripple niece, man that just made me chuckle inside. Anyway, until next time."

"Thanks Charlie, that was fantastic, more than we could have hoped for."

"It was a pleasure, same time next week then?"

"Yes Charlie, we appreciate your time. Once again, thank you."

THANK YOU

COMING SOON

A SPECIAL RELATIONSHIP.

HARRISON JONES, HIS WIFE AND FOUR CHILDREN ALONG WITH HIS DAUGHTER'S BOYFRIEND VISIT LONDON FROM THE UNITED STATES. FOR HARRISON JONES IT IS A HOLIDAY HE HAS DREAMED ABOUT SINCE HE WAS A CHILD. THE DREAM SOON BECOMES TERROR AS HE AND HIS FAMILY FIGHT FOR THEIR LIVES.

WHO WILL SURVIVE?

LLOYD SMITH

Fucked in the Rear

Printed in Great Britain
by Amazon

32460506R00066